Elmore Leonard

MR. MAJESTYK

"A lean, mean thriller. . . . Leonard is one of the crime genre's great writers."
—*Dallas Morning News*

"Leonard is the best in the business: His dialogue snaps, his characters are more alive than most of the people you meet on the street, and his twisting plots always resolve themselves with a no-nonsense plausibility."
—*Newsday*

"Nobody but nobody on the current scene can match his ability to serve up violence so light-handedly, with so supremely deadpan a flourish."
—*Detroit News*

"A gutsy performance by Elmore Leonard."
—*New York Times Book Review*

Also by Elmore Leonard

FICTION

NONFICTION

ELMORE LEONARD

MR. MAJESTYK

WILLIAM MORROW
An Imprint of HarperCollinsPublishers

This book is a work of fiction. The characters, incidents, and dialogue are drawn from the author's imagination and are not to be construed as real. Any resemblance to actual events or persons, living or dead, is entirely coincidental.

HarperCollins books may be purchased for educational, business, or sales promotional use. For information please write: Special Markets Department, HarperCollins Publishers, 10 East 53rd Street, New York, NY 10022.

FIRST HARPERTORCH PAPERBACK PUBLISHED 2002.
FIRST WILLIAM MORROW PAPERBACK PUBLISHED 2012.

Library of Congress Cataloging-in-Publication Data has been applied for.

ISBN 978-0-06-218840-3

12 13 14 15 16   OV/RRD   10 9 8 7 6 5 4 3 2 1

1

THIS MORNING they were here for the melons: about
sixty of them waiting patiently by the two stake
trucks and the old blue-painted school bus. Most of
them, including the few women here, were Chicano
migrants, who had arrived in their old junk cars
that were parked in a line behind the trucks. Others, the Valley Agricultural Workers Association
had brought out from Phoenix, dropping them off
at 5:30 A.M. on the outskirts of Edna, where the
state road came out of the desert to cross the U.S.
highway. The growers and the farm workers called
it Junction. There was an Enco gas station on the
corner, then a storefront with a big V.A.W.A. sign
in the window that was the farm labor hiring hall—
closed until next season—and then a café-bar with
a red neon sign that said BEER-WINE. The rest of the
storefronts in the block were empty—dark, gutted
structures that were gradually being destroyed by
the desert wind.

The farm workers stood around on the sidewalk

waiting to be hired, waiting for the labor contractors to finish their coffee, finish talking to the foremen and the waitresses, and come out and point to them and motion them toward the stake trucks and the blue-painted school bus.

The dozen or so whites were easy to spot. Most of them were worn-out looking men in dirty, worn-out clothes that had once been their own or someone else's good clothes. A tight little group of them was drinking Thunderbird, passing the wine bottle around in a paper bag. A couple of them were sipping from beer cans. Two teenaged white boys with long hair stood off by themselves, hip-cocked, their arms folded over tight white T-shirts, not seeming to mind the early morning chill. They would look around casually and squint up at the pale sky.

The Chicanos, in their straw hats and baseball caps, plaid shirts, and Levis or khakis, with their lunch in paper bags, felt the chill. They would look at the sky knowing it was near the end of the season and soon most of them would be heading for California, to the Imperial and San Joaquin valleys. Some of them—once in a while for something to do—would shield their faces from the light and look in the window of the hiring hall, at the rows of folding chairs, at the display of old V.A.W.A. strike posters and yellowed newspaper pages with columns marked in red. They would stare at the photograph of Emiliano Zapata on the wall behind the counter, at the statue of the Virgin Mary on a stand, and try to read the hand-lettered announcements: *Todo el mundo está invitado que venga a la resada*—

Larry Mendoza came out of the café-bar with a carry-out cup of coffee in each hand—one black, one cream and sugar—and walked over to the curb, beyond the front of the old blue-painted school bus. Some of the farm workers stared at him—a thin, bony-shouldered, weathered-looking Chicano in clean Levis and high-heeled work boots, a Texas straw funneled low over his eyes— and one of them, also a Chicano, said, "Hey, Larry, tell Julio you want me. Tell him write my name down at the top." Larry Mendoza glanced over at the man and nodded, but didn't say anything.

Another one said, "How much you paying, Larry? Buck forty?"

He nodded again and said, "Same as everybody." He felt them watching him because he was foreman out at Majestyk and could give some of them jobs. He knew how they felt, hoping each day to get their names on a work list. He had stood on this corner himself, waiting for a contractor to point to him. He had started in the fields for forty cents an hour. He'd worked for sixty cents, seventy-five cents. Now he was making eighty dollars a week, all year: he got to drive the pickup any time he wanted and his family lived in a house with an inside toilet. He wished he could hire all of them, assure each man right now that he'd be working today, but he couldn't do that. So he ignored them, looking down the sidewalk now toward the Enco station where the attendant was pumping gas into an old-model four-wheel-drive pickup that was painted yellow, its high front end pointing this way. Larry Mendoza stood like that, his back to the school bus and the farm workers, waiting, then began to sip the coffee with cream and sugar.

The Enco gas station attendant, with the name *Gil* stitched over the pocket of his shirt, watched the numbers changing in the window of the pump and began to squeeze the handle of the nozzle that curved into the gas tank filler, slowing the rotation of the numbers, easing them in line to read three dollars even, and pulled the nozzle out of the opening.

When he looked over at the station he saw the guy who owned the pickup stepping out of the Men's Room, coming this way across the pavement—a dark, solemn-faced man who might have passed for a Chicano except for his name. Vince Majestyk. Hard-looking guy, but always quiet, the few times he had been there. Vincent Majestyk of MAJESTYK BRAND MELONS that was lettered on the doors of the pickup and made him sound like a big grower. Shit, he looked more like a picker than a grower. Maybe a foreman, with his khaki pants and blue shirt. From what the station attendant had heard about him, the guy was scratching to get by and probably wouldn't be around very long. Comes in, buys three bucks worth of gas. Big deal.

He said, "That's all you want?"

The guy, Majestyk, looked over at him as he walked past the front of the pickup. "If you're not too busy you can wipe the bugs off the windshield," he said, and kept going, over toward the school bus and the farm workers crowding around.

The gas station attendant said to himself, Shit. Get up at five in the morning to sell three bucks' worth. Wait around all day and watch the tourists drive by. Four-thirty sell the migrants each a buck's worth. Shit.

Larry Mendoza handed Majestyk the cup of black coffee and the two of them stood watching as Julio Tamaz, a labor contractor, looked over the waiting groups of farm workers, called off names and motioned them to the school bus. There were already men aboard, seated, their heads showing in the line of windows.

"We're almost ready to go," Mendoza said.

"Good ones?" Majestyk took a sip of coffee.

"The best he's got."

"Bob Santos," the labor contractor called out. "And . . . Anbrocio Verrara."

"They're good," Mendoza said.

"Luis Ortega!"

A frail old man grinned and hurried toward the bus.

"Wait a minute," Mendoza said. "I don't know him. He ever picked before?"

Julio Tamaz, the labor contractor, turned to them with a surprised look. "Luis? All his life. Man, he was conceived in a melon field." Julio's expression brightened, relaxed in a smile as he looked at Majestyk. "Hey, Vincent, nice to see you."

Mendoza said, "That's thirty. We want any more'n that?"

Majestyk was finishing his coffee. He lowered the cup. "If Julio's got any like to work for nothing."

"Man," Julio said, "you tight with the dollar. Like to squeeze it to death."

"How's my credit?"

"Vincent"—Julio's expression was sad now—"I told you. What do I pay them with?"

"All right, I just wondered if you'd changed your mind." He took a fold of bills out of his pants pocket and handed them to the labor contractor. "Straight buck forty an hour, ten hours' work for a crew of thirty comes to four hundred and twenty. Don't short anybody."

Julio seemed offended now. "I take my percent. I don't need to cheat them."

"Larry'll ride with you," Majestyk said. "He finds anybody hasn't slipped honeydew melons before, they come back with you and we get a refund. Right?"

"Man, I never give you no bums. These people all experts."

Majestyk had already turned away and was walking back to the Enco station.

The attendant with the name *Gil* on his shirt was standing by the pickup.

"That's three bucks."

Majestyk reached into a back pocket for his wallet this time. He took out a five-dollar bill and handed it to the attendant, who looked at the bill and then at Majestyk. Without a word he turned and leisurely walked off toward the station. Majestyk watched him for a moment, knowing the guy was going to make him wait. He walked off after the guy and followed him into the station, but still had to wait while the guy fooled around at the cash register, shifting bills around in the cash drawer and breaking open a roll of coins.

"Take your time," Majestyk said.

When the bell rang he turned to see a car pulling into the station: an old-model Ford sedan that was faded blue-purple and rusting out, and needed a muffler. He watched the people getting out, moving slowly, stretching and looking around. There seemed to be more of them than the car could hold.

The station attendant was saying, "I'm short of singles. I'll have to give you some change."

There were five of them, four men in work clothes and a young woman, migrants, looking around, trying to seem at ease. The young woman took a bandana from her head and, raising her face in the sunlight, closing her eyes, shook her hair from side to side, freeing it in the light breeze that came across the highway stirring sand dust. She was a good-looking girl, nice figure in pants and a T-shirt, in her early twenties, or maybe even younger. Very good-looking. Not self-conscious now, as though she was alone with whatever was behind her closed eyes. Two of the men went to the pop machine digging coins out of their pockets.

Beyond the girl the blue-painted school bus passed the station and the state road intersection, moving east down the highway.

"Here you are," the attendant said.

Majestyk held out his hand and the attendant dropped eight quarters into his palm, four at a time.

"Three, that's four and five. Hurry back and see us now."

Majestyk didn't say anything. He gave the guy a little smile. He had enough to think about and wasn't going to let the guy bother him. When he turned to the doorway he had to stop short. The girl, holding the bandana, was coming in and their eyes met for a moment—nice eyes, brown—before she looked past him toward the attendant.

"Is there a key you have to the Ladies' Room?"

The attendant's eyes moved past her, to the four men outside, and back again. "No, it's broken, you can't use it. Go down the road someplace."

"Maybe it's all right now," the girl said. "Have you looked at it? Sometimes they get all right by themselves."

The attendant was shaking his head now. "I'm telling you it's broken. Take my word for it and go someplace else, all right?"

"What about the other one?" the girl said. "The Men's Room."

"It's broken too. Both of 'em are broken."

"See, we go in separately," the girl went on. "The men, they come out, then I go in. So you don't have to call the cops, say we're doing it in there."

"I can call the cops right now." The attendant's voice was louder, irritated. "I'm telling you both toilets are broken. You got to go someplace else."

"Where do you go?" the girl said. She waited a moment, not looking around but knowing the four men were close to the doorway now, and could hear her.

The attendant said, "I'm warning you—"

And the girl said, "Maybe you never go, uh? That's why you're full of shit."

The migrants grinned, some of them laughed out loud and there were words in Spanish, though the girl continued to stare at the attendant calmly, almost without expression.

The attendant turned to a counter and came around with a wrench in his hand, his jaw set tightly. Majestyk reached over to put a hand on the man's arm.

He said, "When did the toilet break? Since I used it?"

"Listen, I got to do what I'm told." He pulled his arm away from Majestyk and lowered his voice then, though the tension was still there. "Like anybody else. The boss says don't let no migrants in the toilets. He says I don't care they dancing around like they can taste it, don't let them in the toilets. They go in there, mess up the place, piss all over, take a bath in the sink, use all the towels, steal the toilet paper, man, it's like a bunch of pigs was in there. Place is filthy, I got to clean up after."

"Let them use it," Majestyk said.

"I tell you what my boss said. Man, I can't do nothing about it."

"What're they supposed to do?"

"Go out in the bushes, I don't know. Mister, you have any idea how many migrants stop here?"

"I know what they can do," Majestyk said. He turned from the attendant to the nice-looking Chicano girl, noticing now that she was wearing small pearl earrings.

"He says for all of you to come inside."

"I want them out of here!"

"He says he's sorry the toilets are broken."

"They're always broken," the girl said. "Every place they keep the broken toilets locked up so nobody steal them."

Majestyk was looking at her again. "You come here to work?"

"For the melons or whatever time it is. Last month we were over at Yuma."

"You know melons, uh?"

"Melons, onions, lettuce, anything you got."

"You want to work today?"

The girl seemed to think about it and then shrugged and said, "Yeah, well, since we forgot our golf clubs we might as well, uh?"

"After you go to the bathroom." Majestyk's gaze, with the soft hint of a smile, held on her for another moment.

"First things first," the girl said.

"Listen, I don't say they can't use them," the attendant said now. "You think I own this place? I work here."

"He says he works here," Majestyk said.

The girl nodded. "We believe it."

"And he says since the toilets are broken you can

use something else." Majestyk's gaze moved away, past the attendant and the shelves of lube oil and the cash register and the coffee and candy machines, taking in the office.

"What're you doing?" The attendant was frowning, staring at him. "Listen, they can't use something else. They got to get out of here."

Majestyk's gaze stopped, held for a moment before coming back to the attendant. "He says use the wastebasket if you want," and motioned to the migrants with his hands. "Come on. All of you, come on in."

As two of the migrants came in hesitantly behind the girl, grinning, enjoying it, and the other two moved in closer behind her, the attendant said, "Jesus Christ, you're crazy! I'm going to call the police, that's what I'm going to do."

"Try and hold on to yourself," Majestyk said to him quietly. "You don't own this place. You don't have to pay for broken windows or anything. What do you care?"

The phone was on the desk in front of him, but the Enco gas station man with *Gil* over his shirt pocket, who had never been farther away from this place than Phoenix, hesitated now, afraid to reach for the phone or even look at it. What would happen if he did? Christ, what was going on here? He didn't know this guy Vincent Majestyk. Christ, a cold, quiet guy, he didn't know anything about him except he grew melons. He'd hardly ever seen him before.

"How do you want it?" Majestyk said to the attendant.

Watching him, the migrants were grinning, beginning to glance at each other, confident of this man for no reason they knew of but feeling it, enjoying it, stained and golden smiles softening dark faces and bringing life to their eyes, expressions that separated them as individuals able to think and feel, each one a person now, each one beginning to laugh to himself at this gas station man and his boss and his wastebasket and his toilets he could keep locked or shove up his ass for all they cared. God, it was good; it was going to be something to tell about.

"Let them use the toilets," Majestyk said to the attendant. "All right?"

The attendant held on another moment, as if thinking it over, letting them know he was not being forced into anything but was making up his own mind. He shrugged indifferently then and nodded to two keys that were attached to flat pieces of wood and hung from the wall next to the door.

"Keys're right there," the attendant said. "Just don't take all day."

2

THE GIRL RODE with him in the pickup and the four men followed in the Ford sedan that needed a paint job and a muffler, heading east on the highway toward the morning sun, seeing the flat view of sand and scrub giving way to sweeps of green fields on both sides of the highway, citrus and vegetable farms, irrigation canals and, in the near distance, stands of trees that bordered the fields and marked back roads and dry washes. Beyond the trees, in the far distance, a haze of mountains stood low against the sky, forming a horizon that was fifty miles away, in another world.

The girl was at ease, though every once in a while she would turn and look through the back window to make sure the car was still following.

Finally Majestyk said, "I'm not going to lose them."

"I'm not worried about that," the girl said. "It's the car. It could quit on them any time, blow a tire or something."

"They relatives of yours?"

"Friends. We worked the same place at Yuma."

"How long you been traveling together?"

The girl looked at him. "What are you trying to find out? If I sleep with them?"

"I'm sorry. I was just curious, I didn't mean to offend you."

When she spoke again her tone was quiet, the hostility gone. "We go to different places, help organize the farm workers. But we have to stop and work to pay our way."

"You're with the union?"

"Why? I tell you, yes, then you don't hire us?"

"You sure get on the muscle easy. I don't care if you're union or not, long as you know melons."

"Intimately. I've been in the fields most of my life."

"You sound like you went to school though."

"Couple of years. University of Texas, El Paso. I took English and History and Economics. Psychology 101. I went to the football games, learned all the cheers. Yeaaa, team—" Her voice trailed off and she added, quietly, "Shit."

"I never went past high school," Majestyk said.

"So you didn't waste any time."

He looked at her again, interested, intrigued. "You haven't told me your name."

"Nancy Chavez. I'm not related to the other Chavez, but I'll tell you something. I was on the picket line with them at Delano, during the grape strike."

"I believe it."

"I was fifteen."

He glanced at her and waited again, because she seemed deep in thought. Finally he said, "Are you from California?"

"Texas. Born in Laredo. We moved to San Antonio when I was little."

"Yeah? I was at Fort Hood for a while. I used to get down to San Antone pretty often."

"That's nice," Nancy Chavez said.

He looked at her again, but didn't say anything. Neither of them spoke until they were passing melon fields and came in sight of the packing shed, a long wooden structure that looked like a warehouse. It was painted yellow, with MAJESTYK BRAND MELONS written across the length of the building in five-foot bright green letters.

As the pickup slowed down, approaching a dirt road adjacent to the packing shed, the girl said, "That's you, uh?"

"That's me," Majestyk said.

The pickup turned off the highway onto the dirt road and passed the front of the packing shed. There were crates stacked on the loading dock, the double doors were open; but there was no sign of activity, the shed stood dark and empty. Next to it was a low frame building with a corrugated metal roof that resembled an army barracks. The girl knew what it was, or what it had been—living quarters for migrants. It was also empty, some of its windows broken, its white paint peeling, fading gray.

The farmhouse was next, another fifty yards down the road, where three small children—two boys and a little girl—were standing in the hard-packed yard, watching the pickup drive past, and a woman was hanging wash on a clothesline that extended out from the side of the house. The children waved and Nancy put her hand out the window to wave back at them.

"Are they yours, too?"

"My foreman, Larry Mendoza's," Majestyk said. "That's my house way down there, by the trees."

She could see the place now, white against the dark stand of woods, a small, one-story farmhouse with a porch, almost identical to the foreman's house. She could see the blue school bus standing in the road ahead and, off to the left beyond the ditch, the melon fields, endless rows of green vines that were familiar to the girl and never changed, hot dusty rows that seemed to reach from Texas to California, and were always waiting to be picked.

"You must have a thousand acres," she said. "More than that."

"A hundred and sixty. The man that owned this

land used to have a big operation, but he sub-divided when he sold out. This is my second crop year, and if I don't make it this time—"

When he stopped, the girl said, "What?"

She turned to see him staring straight ahead through the windshield, at the school bus they were approaching and the men standing in the road. She could see the car now, a new model of some kind shining golden in the sunlight, parked beyond the bus. Beyond the car was a stake truck. At the same time she was aware of the figures out in the melon field, at least twenty or more, stooped figures dotted among the rows.

She said, "You have two crews working?"

"I only hired one," Majestyk said.

"Then who's out there working?"

He didn't answer her. He pulled up behind the bus and got out without wasting any time, feeling a tenseness now as he walked past the bus, past the faces in the windows, and saw Larry Mendoza's serious, concerned expression. His foreman stood with Julio Tamaz by the front of the bus, both of them watching him, anxious. Only a few of Julio's crew had gotten out. The rest of them were still inside wondering, as he was, what the hell was going on.

He was aware of the two men standing by the gold Dodge Charger that was parked on the left side of the road—long hair and Mexican bandit moustaches, one of them wearing sunglasses. A skinny, hipless guy with a big metal belt buckle, bright yellow shirt and cowboy boots, watching him, seeming unconcerned, lounged against the rear deck of the Charger with his arms folded. There was another guy he had never seen before standing by the stake truck that, he noticed now, had a horn-type speaker mounted on the roof of the cab.

"We get here," Larry Mendoza said, "this guy's already got a crew working."

Julio Tamaz said, "What are we supposed to do, Vincent, go home? Man, what is this?"

Majestyk walked over to the ditch, behind the Charger, and stood looking out at the field, at the men standing among the rows with long burlap sacks hanging from their shoulders. Only a few of them were working. All of them, he noticed, were white. And all of them, that he could make out clearly, had the same worn-out, seedy look, skid row bums taken from the street and dropped in a melon field.

But not my melon field, Majestyk was saying to himself. He turned to the skinny dude with sunglasses lounged against the car.

"I don't think I know you."

He watched the guy straighten with a lazy effort and come off the car extending his hand.

"I'm Bobby Kopas. Come out from Phoenix with some top hand pickers for you."

Majestyk ignored the waiting hand. "I don't think I've ever done business with you either. What I know for sure is I never will."

Bobby Kopas grinned at him, letting his hand fall. " 'Fore you say anything you might be sorry about—how does a buck twenty an hour sound to you? Save yourself some money and they're already hard at it."

"I hire who I want," Majestyk said. "I don't hire a bunch of winos never slipped melons before."

Kopas glanced over at the bus, at Larry Mendoza and Julio and Nancy Chavez. "I don't know—you hire all these Latins, no white people. Looks like discrimination to me."

"Call them out and get off my land," Majestyk said.

"These Latins buddies of yours? What do you care who does the job, long as it gets done?"

"I just told you, I hire who I want."

"Yeah, well the thing is you want me," Kopas said. "Only it hasn't sunk in your head yet. Because everything is easier and less trouble when you hire my crew. If you understand what I'm saying to you."

There it was, a little muscle-flexing. Hotshot dude trying to pressure him, sure of himself, with two strong-arm guys to back him up. Majestyk stared at him and thought about it and finally he said, "Well, you're making sounds like you're a mean little ass-kicker. Only you haven't convinced me yet it's true. Then again, if you say anything else and I don't like it, I'm liable to take your head off. So maybe you ought to consider that."

Majestyk stared at him a moment, as Kopas began to say, "Now hang on a minute, dad—" but that was all. Majestyk turned away, ignoring him, looking out at the field again and began yelling at the winos.

"Come on, time to go home! Leave anything you picked or messed up and haul ass out, right now! Come on, gents, move it!"

The few that were working stopped, straightened, and now all of the men in the rows were looking this way, not sure what to do. Kopas saw them. He had to stop them before they moved. He turned to the guy behind him and nodded toward the stake truck. The guy took off. The other one, standing by the truck, saw him coming and quickly got into the cab.

"You hear me?" Majestyk yelled out. "Time to go home. Man made a mistake. You come to the wrong place." As he began to say, "Come on, move!" his words were drowned out by a blast of rock music, intense hard rock, the sound of electrified, amplified guitars wailing out over the melon fields.

Majestyk looked toward the truck, at the horn speaker mounted on the cab. His gaze shifted to Bobby Kopas. He saw him grinning and saw the grin fade as he moved toward him. He saw him get around to the side of the Charger, reach in through the open window and come out with a pump-action shotgun. Kopas put the gun under his arm, pointing down slightly, holding it with both hands, and Majestyk stopped.

Nancy Chavez, staring at Bobby Kopas, came away from the bus. She said, "Man, what're you going to do now, shoot us?"

"I'm gonna talk to him and this time he's gonna listen," Kopas said. "That's what I'm gonna do."

She was moving toward him, taking her time. "Buck twenty an hour—you going to shoot people for that? Man, you need another hit of something."

"He threatened me," Kopas said, "and all your people heard it. But I'll tell you, he ain't gonna threaten me again."

Staring at him, moving toward him, Nancy Chavez said, "I don't know—guy brings wine heads out, plays music for them. He must be a little funny."

Majestyk was past the trunk of the car, two strides from the muzzle of the shotgun.

"You say you come from Phoenix? What do you do there, roll drunks and hire them as pickers?"

Kopas kept his eyes on him, holding onto the shotgun. "I'm telling you, keep back. Stay where you are."

"Mean little ass-kicker like you," Majestyk said. "What do you need a gun for?"

"I'm warning you!"

Majestyk stepped into him as he brought the shotgun up, grabbing the barrel with his left hand, and drove his right fist hard into Bobby Kopas's face, getting some nose and mouth, staying with him as Kopas went back against the car door, and slammed the fist into him again, getting his sunglasses this time, wiping them from his face, and pulling the shotgun out of his hands as Kopas twisted and his head and shoulders fell into the window opening.

The other one with the hair and heavy moustache who had been with Kopas was coming back from the truck, coming fast, but not in time. He stopped and raised his hands, three yards away, as Majestyk put the shotgun on him.

The loud rock music continued, the wailing guitars wailed on, until Majestyk stepped into the middle of the road, raised the shotgun and blew the horn speaker off the top of the stake truck.

The sound stopped. Majestyk looked at the man

with his hands half raised. He pumped a shell into the chamber of the shotgun and walked past him to the truck. When he opened the rightside door he could hear the radio music again, the rock guitars. The man sitting behind the wheel stared at him.

"Get those wine heads out of my field," Majestyk said, and slammed the door.

He came back to the Charger, nodded toward Kopas hanging against the door and said to the one with his hands raised, "Put him inside and get out of here." He waited, seeing the blood coming out of Kopas's nose, staining his yellow shirt, as the guy pulled Kopas around, opened the door and eased him onto the seat.

"You got the key?" When the guy nodded Majestyk said, "Open the trunk."

He had to wait for him again, for the guy to walk back and unlock it. As the trunk lid swung up, Majestyk stepped over, threw the shotgun inside and slammed it closed. He stood one stride away from the guy with the hair and the heavy moustache who was staring at him and maybe was on the verge of doing something.

Majestyk said, "Make up your mind."

The guy hesitated; but the moment was there and passed. He walked around to the driver's side and got in the car.

Majestyk walked up on the other side to look at

Kopas holding a handkerchief to his face. He said, "Hey," and waited for Kopas to lower the handkerchief and look out at him.

"You want my opinion, buddy, I think you're in the wrong business."

3

HE WAS ARRESTED that afternoon.

Nancy Chavez saw it happen. She was crouched in the vines working a row, slipping the ripe honeydew melons off, gently turning the ones that would be ready in a day or two, pushing them under the vines so they would not be exposed to the sun. Her sack, with the rope loop digging into her shoulder, was almost full. A few more melons and she would carry it over to the road and hand it up to Vincent Majestyk in the trailer that was hooked to the pickup truck. Maybe they would talk a little bit while he unloaded the sack and she got a drink of water from the canvas bag that hung from the side of the trailer. He had been curious about her, admitting it, and she was curious about him. There were questions in her mind, though she wasn't sure she could come right out and ask them. She wondered if he lived alone or had a wife somewhere. She wondered if he knew what he was doing, if he could harvest a hundred and sixty acres within the next week, sort and pack the melons and get them to a broker. Even for a late crop he was running out of time.

When her sack was full and she looked up again, straightening, the squad car, with blue lights flashing, was standing in the road by the pickup truck. She saw the two policemen, in khaki uniforms and cowboy hats, talking to Majestyk in the trailer. When he came down and one of them took him by the arm, he pulled his arm free and the other policeman moved in close with his hand on his holster. What the hell was going on?

Nancy Chavez dropped the sack and started across the rows. Some of the other pickers were watching now and Larry Mendoza was coming out of the field, not far away from her. She hurried, but by the time she and Mendoza reached the road, Majestyk was in the squad car and it was moving off, blue lights spinning, raising a column of dust that thinned to nothing by the time the squad car reached the highway and turned left, toward Edna.

"What's going on?" Nancy Chavez said. "They arresting him?"

Larry Mendoza shook his head, squinting in the sun glare. "I don't know. But I guess somebody better go find out."

"Is there somebody at his house maybe you better tell?"

"No, there's nobody lives there but him."

"He isn't married?"

"Not anymore."

The squad car was out of sight but Mendoza was still staring in the direction of the highway. "Those were sheriff's deputies. Well, I guess I better go find out."

"If there's anything you want me to do," the girl said, "don't be afraid to tell me. Go on, we'll take care of the melons."

The Edna post of the County Sheriff's Department had been remodeled and painted light green. Everything was light green, the cement block walls, the metal desks, the chairs, the Formica counter—light green and chrome-trimmed under bright fluorescent lights. They took Majestyk into an office, sat him down against the wall and left him.

After a while one of the arresting officers came back in with a file folder, sat down at a desk where there was a typewriter and began to peck at the keys with two fingers. The deputy's name was Harold Ritchie. He was built like a running guard, had served four years in the Marines, including a combat tour in Vietnam, and had a tattoo on his right forearm, a snake coiled around a dagger, with an inscription that said *Death Before Dishonor*.

Looking down at the typewriter, as if reciting the words from memory, he said, "This warrant states that you have been arrested on a charge that constitutes a felony, assault with a deadly weapon. You may choose to stand mute at this time and of course you have a right to counsel. You can call a lawyer or anybody you want. You are allowed one phone call—"

The deputy paused, looking up, as a man in a lightweight summer suit came into the office and closed the door behind him.

The man said, "Go on. Don't let me interrupt."

His tone was mild, his appearance slightly rumpled. For some reason he reminded Majestyk of a schoolteacher, a man who had taught high school English or civics for at least thirty years, though he knew the man was a policeman.

"After which," Ritchie continued, "you will be released on bond, if you choose, or held here till you're taken to the county seat for your pretrial examination."

The deputy looked up, finished. The mild-appearing man came over to the desk, his gaze holding on Majestyk.

"My name is Detective Lieutenant McAllen. Do you understand your rights under the law?"

"I can keep my mouth shut, and that seems about it," Majestyk said.

"You can tell your side of it if you want. Feel free."

"A man I never saw before tried to force me to use a crew I didn't need."

"So you hit him with a shotgun."

"I hit him with a fist."

"The complainant says he was offering you a business proposition. Instead of a simple no thanks, you assaulted him with a shotgun."

"It was his, not mine," Majestyk said. "Man was trespassing on my land."

"Lieutenant"—the deputy was holding the file folder; he handed it, open, to McAllen—"four years ago in California he got one to five for assault. Served a year in Folsom."

McAllen studied the folder a moment before looking up. "Vincent A. Majestyk. What're you, a Polack?"

Majestyk stared at him in silence. The lieutenant was looking at the folder again.

"He grows melons," the deputy said. "Generally keeps to himself. I mean he hasn't given us any trouble before this."

"But sometimes you like to mix it up," McAllen said. "You use a gun the time in California?"

"I was in a bar. A man hit me with a beer bottle."

"Sitting there minding your own business, he hit you with a bottle."

"We were arguing about something. He wanted to go outside. I told him to drink his beer."

"So he hit you and you hit him back. If it was your first offense, how come they put you away?"

"The guy was in the hospital a while," Majestyk said. "He came to the trial with a broken collarbone and his jaw wired up and some buddies of his that said I started it and kicked his face in when he was on the floor."

"But you never did such a thing."

"I've already been tried for it. You want to do it again?"

"Served your time and now making an honest living. You married?"

"I was four years. My wife divorced me while I was in prison."

"Run out on you, huh? How come? Didn't you get along?"

"You want to talk about my marriage? Find out what we did in bed?"

McAllen didn't say anything for a moment. He stared at Majestyk, then turned to leave, dropping the folder on the desk.

"I think you better talk to a lawyer."

"Lieutenant, I got a crop of melons to get in." He saw the man hesitate and turn to look at him again. "Let me get them picked, I'll come back right after."

McAllen took his time. "That's what you're worried about, melons?"

"I get them in and packed this week or I lose the crop. I'm asking for a few days, that's all."

"The court'll set a bond on you," McAllen said. "Pay it, you can go out and pick all the melons you want."

"Except if I put up bail I won't have any money left for a crew. And I can't pick a hundred and sixty acres by myself."

McAllen was thoughtful again, studying him. He said, "I don't know anything about you but the fact you've been arrested for assault and have a previous conviction. So I don't have any reason to feel sorry for you, do I?"

"I give you my word," Majestyk said. "I'll come right back."

"And even if I did feel sorry for you, if for some reason I believed you, the law doesn't happen to make any provision for your word," McAllen said. "That's how it is." He turned and walked out.

Larry Mendoza waited three and a half hours on the bench by the main desk, looking up every time one of the deputies came out of an office. They would stand around drinking coffee, not paying any attention to him. Finally they told him no, it was too late to see his friend now, he'd have to come back tomorrow. They told him the charge was felonious assault and the bond was set at five thousand, which would cost him five hundred, cash, if he wanted to go to the county seat and get a bondsman to put up the money. Or wait a couple of days for the examination. If the court set a trial date and appointed a lawyer, maybe the lawyer could get the bond lowered.

Christ, he didn't know anything about bonds or examinations. He didn't know what the hell was going on—how they could arrest a man for throwing somebody off his property who didn't belong there. It didn't make sense.

When he got back Julio had already picked up his crew and was gone. He asked his wife, Helen, and Nancy Chavez and the four men who were with her—the group of them sitting on the front steps of his house in the shade—if it made any sense.

Nancy Chavez said, "Cops. Talking to cops is like talking to the wall. They don't tell you anything they don't want to."

Of course not, it didn't make sense. Christ almighty, who ever expected cops to make sense? All they could do was keep working, do that much for him while he was in jail, then all of them tell at the examination, or whatever it was, what happened and maybe, if the judge listened, he would see it didn't make any sense and Vincent would get off. Maybe.

Helen Mendoza let Nancy use her kitchen and gave her some green beans and beets to go with the Franco-American spaghetti she fixed for her friends and herself. Larry Mendoza said why didn't they stay in Vincent's house while he was in jail. Vincent wouldn't mind. In fact he'd want them to. Nancy Chavez said all right, for one night. But tomorrow they'd get the migrant quarters in shape, clean up the kitchen and a couple of rooms and stay there. They had cots and bedding in the car. For a week it wouldn't be so bad. They'd lived in worse places.

Larry Mendoza went back to the Edna Post the next day, Saturday. They searched him good and put him in a little closet of a room that had a table, two chairs facing each other and a metal cabinet. He waited about a half hour before a deputy brought Majestyk in and closed the door. The deputy waited outside. They could see him through the glass part of the door.

"Are you all right? Christ, it doesn't make any sense."

"I'm fine," Majestyk told him. "Listen, what we got to think about's the crop. You're here visiting me, you should be working the crew."

"Man, we're worried about you. What if they put you in jail?"

"I'm already in jail."

"In the penitentiary. For something that don't make any sense."

"We're going to court Monday," Majestyk said. "I'll see if I can talk to the judge, explain it to him."

"And we'll be there," Mendoza said. "Tell them what happened."

"I'll tell them. You'll be out in the field."

"Vincent, you need all the help you can get. You got to have a lawyer."

"I need pickers more than I do a lawyer," Majestyk said, "and they both cost money."

"The deputy says the court will appoint one."

"Maybe. We'll see what happens. But right now, today and tomorrow, the melons are out there, right? And they're not going to wait much longer. You don't get them in we'll lose a crop, two years in a row."

Mendoza was frowning, confused. "How can something like this happen? It doesn't make any sense."

"I don't know," Majestyk said. "If it isn't a drought or a hailstorm it's something else. Skinny little dude comes along thinking he's a big shooter—"

"Bobby Kopas," Mendoza said. "This morning Julio says he saw the guy's car parked at a motel."

"Where?"

"Right here, in Edna. He's still hanging around."

"I can't think about him," Majestyk said. "I would sure like to see him again sometime, but I can't think about him. I do—I'm liable to get it in my head to bust out of here."

Mendoza reached across the table to touch his arm. "Vincent, don't do anything foolish, all right?"

"I'll try not to," Majestyk said.

4

MONDAY MORNING, early, they brought Majestyk and four other prisoners out of the jail area to a tank cell, near the back entrance, that was used for drunks and overnighters. There were no bunks in here, only a varnished bench against two of the light green cement block walls, a washbasin, and a toilet without a seat. The fluorescent lights, built into the ceiling and covered with wire mesh, reflected on the benches and waxed tile floor. For a jail the place was clean and bright; that much could be said for it.

The food wasn't too good though. A trusty, with a deputy standing by, slipped the trays in under the barred section of wall, next to the door. Five trays, for Majestyk, two Chicanos, a black guy, and a dark-haired, dude-looking guy in a suit and tinted glasses who hadn't said a word all morning.

One of the Chicanos passed the trays around and went back to sit with the other Chicano, probably a couple of migrants. The black guy was near the corner, where the two benches met. The dark-haired guy looked at his tray and set it on the bench next to him, between where he was sitting low against the wall and where Majestyk sat with his tray on his lap.

Stiff-looking fried eggs and dried-up pork sausage, stale bread, no butter, and lukewarm coffee. Majestyk ate it, cleaned the tray, because he was hungry. But he'd have a word for the deputy when he saw him again. The one with the tattoo. Ask him if they ruined the food on purpose. Christ, it was just as easy to do it right. Where'd they get the idea food had to be stiff and cold?

He looked down at the tray next to him. The guy hadn't touched anything. He sat with his shoulders hunched against the wall, smoking a cigarette. Long dark wavy hair that almost covered his ears and a two-day growth of beard. Striped collar sticking out of the rumpled, expensive-looking dark suit. Shirt open, no tie. No expression on his face behind the lightly tinted wire-frame glasses.

Looking at him, Majestyk said, "You going to eat your sausage?"

The guy drew on his cigarette. He didn't look at Majestyk. He moved his hand to the tray, behind it, and sent it off the bench to hit with a sharp metal clatter, skidding, spilling over the tile floor.

The two Chicanos and the black guy were poised over their trays, eyes raised, but watching only for a moment before looking down again and continuing to eat.

"You're not going to eat it," Majestyk said, "then nobody does, uh?"

The dark-haired guy was lighting a fresh cigarette from the butt of another, the pack still in his hand.

He said, "You want it? Help yourself."

"I guess not," Majestyk said. He looked at the guy as he put the pack of cigarettes in his coat pocket. "You got an extra one of those?"

The guy didn't say anything. He drew on his cigarette and blew the smoke out slowly.

"I'll pay you back when I get out," Majestyk said. "How'll that be?"

The guy turned now to look at him, and another voice said, "Hey, you want a smoke?"

The black guy was holding up a cigarette package that was almost flat.

Majestyk put his tray on the bench and walked over to him. They both took one and Majestyk sat down next to the black guy to get a light.

"Man, don't you know who that is?"

"Some movie star?"

"That's Frank Renda." The black guy kept his voice low, barely moving his mouth.

"He looks like an accordian player," Majestyk said, "used to be on TV."

"Jesus Christ, I said Frank Renda."

"I don't know—I might've heard of him."

"He's in the rackets. Was a hit man. You know what I'm saying to you? He shoots people, with a gun."

"But they caught him, huh?"

"Been trying to for a long time," the black guy said. "Other night this off-duty cop pulls up in front of a bar, some place up on the highway. He sees a man come out. Sees Renda get out of his car, walk up to the man, and bust him five times with a thirty-eight."

"Why didn't the cop shoot him?"

"Didn't have to. Renda's gun's empty."

"He doesn't sound too bright. Pulling a dumb thing like that."

"They say he wanted the man bad, couldn't wait."

Majestyk was studying Renda. Maybe he was dumb, but he looked cool, patient, like somebody who moved slowly, without wasted effort. He didn't look like an accordian player now. He looked like some of the guys he had seen in prison, at Folsom. Mean, confident, hard-nosed guys who would give you that look no matter what you said to them. Like who the fuck are you? Don't waste my time. How did guys get like that? Always on the muscle.

"They got him this time," the black guy said.

"Gonna nail his ass for ninety-nine years—you ask him is he gonna eat his sausage."

Because of Renda they brought the five prisoners out the back way to the parking area, where the gray county bus and the squad cars were waiting. Get them out quick, without attracting a lot of attention. But a crowd of local people had already gathered, along with the reporters and TV newsmen who had been in Edna the past two days and were ready for them. A cameraman with a shoulder-mounted rig began shooting as soon as the door opened and the deputies began to bring them out in single file, the two Chicanos first, startled by the camera and the people watching, then the black guy. They held up Renda and Majestyk in the hallway inside the door, to handcuff them because they were felons. A deputy told them to put their hands behind their backs; but the deputy named Ritchie told him to cuff them in front—it was a long ride, let them sit back and enjoy it.

When Renda appeared, between two deputies, the TV camera held on him, panning with him to the bus, and a newsman tried to get in close, extending a hand mike.

"Frank, over here. What do you think your chances are? They got a case against you or not?"

Renda held his head low, turned away from the camera. A deputy stuck out his hand, pushing the mike away, and two more deputies moved in quickly, from the steps by the rear door, to stand in the newsman's way and restrain him if they had to. This left Majestyk alone at the top of the steps. He watched them put Renda aboard the bus. Four, five deputies standing now with their backs to him. He watched the newsman with the mike come around and mount the steps. The newsman turned, facing the bus, and the TV camera swung toward him.

Majestyk was close enough to hear him and stood listening as the TV newsman said, "Today, Frank Renda is being taken to the county seat for pretrial examination on a charge that will undoubtedly be first-degree murder. Renda, a familiar name in organized crime, has been arrested nine times without a conviction. Now, it would appear, his luck has finally run out. The prosecutor's office is convinced Renda will stand trial, be convicted of the murder charge, and spend the rest of his life in prison. This is Ron Malone with TV-Action News coming to you from Edna."

Majestyk walked down the steps past the newsman, came up behind the deputies standing by the bus door and said, "Excuse me."

The two deputies nearest him turned, with momentary looks of surprise. One of them took his arm then and said, "Get in there."

He got in, moved past the driver and the deputy standing by him, and took a seat on the left side of the bus, in front of the black guy, who leaned forward as he sat down and said over his shoulder, "You get on TV? Your mama'll be proud to see you."

Renda sat across the aisle, a row ahead of him. The two Chicanos sat together on Renda's side, two rows closer to the front. When the door closed and the bus began to move, circling out of the parking area with a squad car leading and another following, the deputy standing by the driver moved down the aisle to take a seat in the back of the bus. Both he and the driver, Majestyk noticed, were unarmed.

He said to himself, How does that help you? And settled back to stare out the window at the familiar billboards and motels and gas stations, the tacoburger place, the stores that advertised used clothing, *Ropa Usada*. Railroad tracks ran parallel with the highway, beyond a bank of weeds. They passed the warehouses and loading sheds that lined the tracks, platformed old buildings that bore the names of growers and produce companies. They passed the silver water tower that stood against the sky—EDNA, HOME OF THE BRONCOS—and moved out into miles of fences and flat green fields, until the irrigation ditches ended and the subdued land turned color, reverted to its original state, and became desert country.

Looking out at the land he wondered when he would be coming back. When, or if he would be coming back. He said to himself, What are you doing here? How did it happen? Sitting handcuffed in a prison bus. His fields miles behind him. Going to stand trial again. The chance of going to prison again. Could that happen? No, he said to himself, refusing to believe it. He could not let it happen, because he could not live in prison again, ever. He couldn't think about it without the feeling of panic coming over him, the feeling of being suffocated, caged, enclosed by iron bars and cement walls and not able to get out. He remembered reading about a man exploring a cave, hundreds of feet underground, who had crawled into a seam in the rocks and had got wedged there, because of his equipment, and was unable to move forward or backward or reach the equipment with his hands to free it. Majestyk had stopped reading and closed the magazine, because he knew the man had died there.

Prison was for men like Frank Renda—sitting across the aisle with his own thoughts, slouched low in his seat, staring straight ahead, off somewhere in his mind. What was he thinking about?

What difference did it make? Majestyk forgot about Frank Renda and did not look at him again until almost a half hour later, when the land outside the bus had changed again, submitting to signs and gas stations and motels, and the empty highway became a busy street that was taking them through a run-down industrial area on the outskirts of the city.

He noticed Renda because Renda was sitting up straighter now, stretching to see ahead, through the windshield, then turning to look out the windows as the bus moved along in the steady flow of traffic. The man had seemed half asleep before. Now he was alert, as though he was looking for a particular store or building, a man looking for an address written on a piece of paper. Or maybe he had lived around here at one time and it was like revisiting the old neighborhood, seeing what had changed. That was the feeling Majestyk had. He was curious about Renda again and continued to watch him and glance off to follow his gaze. Through the windshield now—to see the intersection they were approaching, the green light and the man standing in the middle of the street, caught between the flows of traffic.

Later, he remembered noticing the man moments before it happened. Maybe ten seconds before— seeing the man in bib overalls holding a paper bag by the neck, a farmer who'd come to town for a bottle of whiskey, guy from the sticks who didn't know how to cross a busy street and got trapped. He remembered thinking that and remembered, vividly, the man in bib overalls waiting for the lead squad car to pass him and then starting across the street, weaving slightly, walking directly into the path of the bus.

There was a screeching sound as the driver slammed on the brakes and the tires grabbed the hot pavement. Majestyk was thrown forward against the seat in front of him, but pushed himself up quickly to see if the man had been hit. No, because the driver was yelling at him. "Goddamn drunk—get out of the way!"

He saw the man's head and shoulders then, past the hood of the bus, the man grinning at the driver.

"Will you get the hell out of the way!"

The deputy who'd been in the rear was coming up the aisle, past Majestyk, and the driver was standing now, leaning on the steering wheel.

The man in the overalls, whose name was Eugene Lundy, was still grinning as he took a .44 Colt magnum out of the paper bag, extended it over the front of the hood, and fired five times, five holes blossoming on the windshield as the driver hit against his seat and went out of it and the deputy was slammed backward down the aisle and hit the floor where Majestyk was standing.

Lundy drew a .45 automatic out of his overalls, turned and fired four times at the squad car that had come to a stop across the intersection. Then he was moving—as the doors of the squad car swung open—past the front of the bus and down the cross street.

Harold Ritchie knocked his hat off getting out of the lead squad car, swinging out of there fast and drawing his big Colt Special. He put it on Lundy, tracking with him, and yelled out for him to halt, concentrating, when he heard his partner call his name.

"Ritch!"

And he looked up to see the panel truck coming like crazy on the wrong side of the street, swerving around from behind the bus to take a sweeping right at the intersection. Ritchie jumped back out of the way, though the truck had room to spare. He saw one of the rear doors open and the bottle with the lighted rag for a wick come flying out and he was moving to the right, running hard, waving an oncoming car to keep back when the bottle smashed against the rear deck of the squad car and burst into flames. Five seconds later the gas tank exploded and instantly the entire car was on fire, inside and out.

Ritchie was across the street now, waving at the traffic, yelling at cars to stop where they were. He didn't see his partner or know where he was. From this angle he could see the second squad car close behind the bus and the driver-side door swing open.

In the same moment he saw the station wagon coming up fast from behind. He saw the shotgun muzzles poke out through the side windows and heard them and saw them go off as the station wagon swerved in, sheared the door off the squad car, and kept coming, beginning a sweeping right turn around the bus.

Ritchie raised his big Colt Special, steadying it beneath the grip with his left hand and squeezed off four shots into the station wagon's windshield. The first two would have been enough, because they hit the driver in the face and the wagon was already out of control, half through the turn when the driver slumped over the wheel and the wagon slammed squarely into the burning squad car.

One of the men in the back seat of the wagon tried to get out the left side and Ritchie shot him before he cleared the doorway. But then he had to reload and the two who went out the other side of the wagon made it to a line of parked cars before Ritchie could put his Colt on them. He still didn't know where his partner was until he got to the station wagon, looked out past the rear end of it and saw his partner lying in the street.

Watching from the bus, Majestyk recognized Ritchie, the one with the tattoo who looked like a pro lineman. He was aiming and firing at two men crouched behind a parked car—until one of them raised up, let go with a shotgun and they took off, running up the street past a line of storefronts. Ritchie stepped out from behind the station wagon, fired two shots that shattered two plateglass windows, then lowered his Colt and started after them, waving his arm again, yelling at the people on the sidewalk and pressed close to the buildings to get inside, to get the hell off the street.

Now there were no police in front of the bus.

The moment Renda moved, Majestyk's gaze was on him, following him up the aisle past the two Chicanos huddled low in their seat. He watched Renda—who did not bother to look at the dead driver lying on the floor—reach past the steering wheel and pull a control level. The door opened. Renda approached it cautiously, looking through the opening and down the cross street a half block to where Eugene Lundy and the panel truck were waiting. He seemed about to step out, then twisted away from the opening, dropping to his hands and knees, as two shots drilled through the pane of glass in the door panel.

Majestyk's gaze came away and he looked down at the deputy lying in the aisle. He was sure the man was dead, but he got out of his seat and reached down to feel for a pulse. Nothing. God, no, the man had been shot through the chest. Majestyk was about to rise, then hesitated as he saw the ring of keys hanging from the deputy's belt. He told himself to do it, *now*, and think about it later if he had to. That's what he did, unhooked the ring and slipped the keys into his pants pocket. As he rose, turning toward the rear of the bus, he saw the black guy, only a few feet away, staring at him.

Neither of them spoke. The black guy looked away and Majestyk moved down the aisle to the back windows.

The second squad car was close behind, directly below him. He could see the deputy behind the wheel, his face bloody, talking excitedly into the radio mike. The next moment he was out of the car with his revolver drawn, moving around the back end of it to the sidewalk. Majestyk watched him. The deputy ran in between two cars that were facing out of a used car lot, then down behind the row of gleaming cars with prices painted on the windshields to where his partner was covering the door of the bus from behind the end car in the line.

Majestyk made his way back up the aisle in a crouch, watching the used car lot through the right-side windows. He saw both deputies raise their revolvers and fire.

With the closely spaced reports Renda dropped again away from the door and behind the first row of seats.

Halfway up the aisle Majestyk watched him.

Renda was looking at the two Chicanos now who were also crouched in the aisle, close to each other with their shoulders hunched.

After a moment Renda said, "Come on, let's go. We're getting out of here."

When they realized he was speaking to them the two Chicanos looked at him wide-eyed, frightened to death, and Renda said again, "Come on, move!"

One of the Chicanos said, "We don't want to go nowhere."

"Jesus, you think we're going to talk it over? I said we're going." Renda was reaching for them now, pulling the first one to his feet, then the other one, pushing them past him in the narrow aisleway.

The other Chicano said, "Man, I was drunk driving—I don't run away from that."

And the Chicano who had spoken before was saying, as he was pushed to the front, "Listen, please, they see us coming out they start shooting!"

"That's what we're going to find out," Renda said.

He crowded them, jamming them in the doorway, then put a foot behind the second man—as the man said, "Please, don't! We don't want to go!"—pushed hard and the two Chicanos were out of the bus, stumbling, getting to their feet, starting to make a run for it.

Majestyk watched the two deputies in the used car lot swing their revolvers over to cover them and was sure they were going to fire. But now the two Chicanos were running toward them with their hands raised high in the air, screaming, "Don't shoot! Please! Don't shoot!" And the deputies lowered their revolvers and waved them into the used car lot.

Renda was watching, crouched by the open door as Majestyk came the rest of the way up the aisle.

"Go out there, you give yourself up or get shot," Majestyk said.

Renda looked over his shoulder at him. He watched Majestyk step over the dead driver and slip into the seat, lean against the steering wheel and reach with both hands to turn on the ignition.

"What're you doing?"

Majestyk didn't answer him. He put the bus in gear, began to ease it forward a few feet, then braked and shifted into reverse.

The two deputies in the used car lot saw it happen. They moved the two Chicanos out of the way and returned their attention to the bus—in time to see it start up abruptly in reverse and smash its high rear end into the grille of their squad car. The bus moved forward—God almighty—went into reverse and again slammed into the car, cranked its wheels and made a U-turn out of there, leaving the radiator of the squad car spewing water and the two deputies watching it pick up speed, back the way they had come. They wanted to shoot. They were ready, but at the last moment had to hold their fire because of the people in cars and on the sidewalk, on the other side of the street.

Then the two city police cars were approaching the intersection from the south—off to the left—their sirens wailing, and the two deputies ran out to the sidewalk, waving their arms to flag the cars down.

Majestyk heard the sirens, the sound growing fainter, somewhere behind them. He headed west on the street they had taken into town, turned north on a side street, then west again a few blocks up. Finally he slowed down and eased the bus into an alley, behind a row of cinderblock industrial buildings that appeared deserted. He pulled the lever to open the door and looked around at the black guy.

"Here's your stop."

"Man," the black guy said, "you know where you going? If they don't shoot you?"

Renda was in the aisle, moving toward the black guy. "Come on, Sambo, move it. And take them with you."

Majestyk helped the black guy lift the bodies of the driver and the deputy and ease them out through the narrow doorway. Renda told them to hurry up, for Christ sake, but Majestyk paid no attention to him.

As he got behind the wheel again the black guy, standing outside, said, "Man, what did you do?"

Majestyk looked at him. For a moment he seemed about to say something, then closed the door in the black guy's face and took off down the alley.

Move out fast and try to get to high country before the police set up roadblocks and got their helicopters out. That's what he had to do. Keep to the back roads, working north, get far enough away from the highway and find some good cover.

That's what he did. Found an old sagging feed barn sitting out by itself on a dried-up section of pasture land, pulled the bus inside, and swung the double doors shut to enclose them in dim silence.

Majestyk remained by the crack of vertical light that showed between the doors, looking out in the direction they had come, seeing the dust settling in the sun glare.

Somewhere behind him in the gloom Renda said, "You move, don't you? I figured you for some kind of a local clown, but you move."

Majestyk didn't say anything.

"What'd they bust you for?"

"Assault."

"With what?"

"A shotgun."

"Assault, shit, that's attempted murder. They were going to jam you the same as me."

"Maybe," Majestyk said.

"Maybe? What do you think you're going to do about it?"

"I got an idea might work."

"Listen," Renda said, "we get to a phone we're out of the country before morning. Drive to Mexico, get some passports, we're gone."

His back still to Renda, Majestyk pulled the deputy's keys out of his pocket. He'd almost forgotten about them, hurrying to get out of there, maybe hurrying too fast and not thinking clearly. He would have to slow down a little. Not waste time, but make sure he wasn't doing anything dumb. He listened to Renda as he began to study the keys and select one that would fit his handcuffs.

"I got friends," Renda was saying, "as you noticed, huh? It was set up in a hurry and they blew it. All right, I call some more friends. They get us out of the country, someplace no extradition, and wait and see what happens. I got enough to live on, I mean high, the rest of my life. It won't be home, shit no, but it won't be in the fucking slam either. I couldn't make that. Couple of weeks I'd be sawing my fucking wrists." He paused. "What're you doing?"

Majestyk didn't say anything and Renda came over to him, his face brightening as he saw the keys.

"Jesus, it keeps getting better. You not only move, you think. Give me those, hold your hands up." As he tried the keys in Majestyk's handcuffs he said, "Figure if you take a long chance, get me out of there, it'd be worth something, huh? Okay, you do something for me, I do something for you. Maybe fix it so you can go with me."

Renda snapped the handcuffs open. As Majestyk slipped them off Renda handed him the keys and raised his own hands to be unlocked.

"How's that sound?"

"I think you got it ass-backwards," Majestyk said, returning the keys to his pocket. "I'm not going with you, you're going with me."

He found an old hackamore that did the job. Looping it around the link of the handcuffs, he could pull Renda along by the length of rope, yank on it when Renda resisted, held back, and the cuffs would dig into his hands.

Leaving the feed barn, hauled out into the sunlight, Renda put up a fight, yelling what the fuck was going on, calling him a crazy insane son of a bitch. So he belted Renda, gave him a good one right in the mouth that quieted him down, and brought him along. But, God, he didn't like the look in the man's eyes. The man wanted to kill him and would probably try. So his idea had better turn out to be a good one and come off without any hitches.

All afternoon and into the evening he led Renda

by the hackamore, forcing him to keep up as they moved through the brush country, following dry washes and arroyos that gradually began to climb, reaching toward the high slopes. Majestyk, in his work clothes and heavy work boots, had little trouble; he seemed at home here. He seemed to know what he was doing, where he was going. Renda, in his tailored suit and thin-soled shoes, stumbled along, falling sometimes, getting his sweat-stained face and clothes caked with dust. Majestyk judged the man's endurance and let him rest when he felt he was near the end of it. Then would pull him to his feet again and they would continue on, through brush and pinyon thickets, climbing, angling across high slopes and open meadows.

He brought Renda more than ten miles this way, up into the mountains, and at dusk when they reached the cabin—a crude one-room structure that was part timber and part adobe—he had the feeling Renda would not have gone another ten yards.

"We're home," Majestyk said.

Renda looked at the place with a dull, lifeless expression. "Where are we?"

"Place I use sometimes. Mostly in hunting season."

Inside, he found a kitchen match on a shelf, feeling for it in the dark, and lighted a kerosene lamp that hung from the overhead.

"We got coffee and canned milk. Probably find some soup or some beans. I haven't been up here since spring."

Renda was looking around the room, at the two metal bunks with bare mattresses, the wooden table and two chairs, the cupboard with open shelves that showed a few cans and cobwebs, but were nearly empty. Renda went to the nearest bunk and sat down. Majestyk followed him over, taking the keys from his pocket.

"Hold up your hands."

The man sure looked worn out. Renda raised his arms slowly, too tired to move. But as soon as Majestyk freed one of his hands, Renda came off the bunk, pushing, chopping at Majestyk with hard jabs. It took him by surprise, Renda's fists stinging his face, and he had to back off and set himself before he could go after Renda, jabbing, feinting, then slamming in a hard right that stunned him and dropped him to the bunk. Majestyk put a knee on him and got him handcuffed to the metal frame before he could move again.

It took something out of him. Majestyk had to sit down on the other bunk and rest, get his breath.

There was silence until Renda said, "All right. What do you call this game?"

Majestyk looked over at him. "You'll find out."

"Tomorrow night," Renda said quietly, "we could be in L.A. Stay at a place I know, get some broads in, booze, anything you want to eat or drink, get some new clothes. A couple of days later we're in Mexico. Get a boat, some more broads. I mean like you never seen before. Cruise around, anything you want, it's on the house. You ever have it like that? Anything you want?"

"I been to L.A.," Majestyk said. "I been to Mexico and I been laid."

"Okay, what do you want?"

"I want to get a melon crop in. That's what I want to do." Renda gave him a puzzled look and he added, "I grow melons."

"Hire your work done."

"I hope to. But I got to be there."

"I'll tell you something," Renda said, taking his time. "I've killed seven men with a gun, one with a crowbar, and another guy I threw off a roof. Five stories. Some people I didn't kill but I had it done. Like I can have it done for you, even if I get put away and they let you off. Any way you look at it, you're dead. Unless we go out of here together. Or, we make a deal."

"What kind of deal?"

"Put a price on it. You take the cuffs off, I walk away. What's it cost?" Renda watched him closely. "If you think it's going to be hot out there, all right, you'll have dough, you can go anywhere you want." He paused. "Or if you feel like taking a chance, turn yourself in, you can tell them I got away. Serve some time, come out, the dough's waiting. How much?" He paused again. "You don't know what your price is, do you? Afraid you might be low. All right, I'll tell you what it is. Twenty-five."

"Twenty-five what?"

"Twenty-five thousand dollars."

It was Majestyk's turn to pause. "How would we work it? I mean how would I get the money?"

"You call a Phoenix number," Renda said. "Say you got a message for Wiley. You say where you want the money delivered and where I can be picked up. It's all you have to do."

Majestyk seemed to be thinking about it. He said, "Twenty-five thousand, huh?"

"Tax free."

"Could you go any higher than that?"

Renda grinned. "Getting greedy now. Like what's another five or ten."

"I just wondered."

"Twenty-five," Renda said. "That's your price. A nice round number. Buy yourself a tractor, a new pair of overalls. Put the rest away for your retirement." He waited a moment. "Well, what do you think?"

"You say I call somebody named Wiley," Majestyk said. "What's the number?"

5

THE PAPAGO TRADING POST was a highway novelty store in the desert, about three miles below and east of the hunting cabin. Big red-painted signs on and around the place advertised AUTHENTIC INDIAN SOUVENIRS . . . ARROWHEADS . . . MOCCASINS . . . HOMEMADE CANDY and ICE COLD BEER. There was a Coca-Cola sign, an Olympia sign, and a Coors sign.

Majestyk came down from the cabin about nine in the morning and approached the store from about three hundred yards up the highway, reading the signs and listening for the sounds of oncoming cars. Nobody passed him. He reached the store and went inside.

Beyond the counters displaying the trinkets and souvenirs, the Indian dolls and blankets, and sayings carved on varnished pieces of wood—like, *"There's only one thing money can't buy. Poverty"*—he saw the owner of the place sitting at a counter that was marble and looked like a soda fountain. The man was about sixty, frail-looking with yellowish gray hair. He was having a beer, drinking it from the can.

Approaching him Majestyk said, "I got a flat tire a couple of miles back. No spare."

"That's a shame," the owner said.

"I wonder if I could use your phone. Call a friend of mine."

"Where's he live?"

"Down at Edna."

"That's two bits call Edna."

Majestyk watched him raise the wet-glistening beer can to his mouth.

"I don't have a spare. The truth is, I don't have any money on me."

"Have to trust you then, won't I?"

Majestyk smiled at him. "You trust me for a can of that too?"

When he got his Coors, a sixteen-ounce can, he took it over to the wall phone with him, looked up a number in the Edna directory, and dialed it. He kept his back to the man at the counter. When a voice came on he said, quietly, "I believe you have a Lieutenant McAllen there? . . . Let me speak to him, please."

He waited, looking over at the counter where the owner of the place was watching him, then turned his back to the man and hunched over the phone again.

"This is Vincent Majestyk. You remember we met a few days ago?" He paused, interrupted, then said, "No, I'm downtown in a hotel. Where do you think I am? Listen, why don't you let me talk for a minute, all right?" But he was interrupted again. "Listen to me, will you? I got Frank Renda . . . I said I got him. . . . You want to listen or you want me to hang up? . . . Okay, I got Renda and you got an assault charge against me. Drop it, tear it up, kick it under the rug, and I'll give you Frank Renda."

With the loud sounds coming from the receiver he held the phone away from him, covered the speaker with his hand, and looked over at the owner of the place.

"He's sore cause I took him away from his breakfast." He turned and put the phone to his ear again, waiting to break in.

"Yeah, well nothing's free in this world," Majestyk said finally. "You want him, that's the deal. . . . No, I'll deliver him. You come here you're liable to say you found us. But I bring him in it's me doing it and nobody else. . . . Yeah. Yeah, well it's nice doing business with you too."

He hung up, took a sip of beer, but didn't move away from the phone. "Put another call on there, okay?" he said to the store owner. "Phoenix. And maybe a couple more beers, to go."

He finished dialing, waited, and as he turned to the wall said, "I got a message for somebody named

Wiley. You understand? All right, get a pencil and piece of paper and write down what I tell you."

It was a little after twelve, the sun directly above them, when the sports car appeared on the county road. They had been waiting since eleven-thirty, partway up the slope that was covered with stands of pinyon pine. In that time this was the first car they had seen.

"That's it," Renda said. He started to rise, awkwardly, still handcuffed.

Majestyk motioned to him. "Keep down." He watched the sports car, a white Jaguar XK, go by raising a trail of dust on the gravel road, finally reaching a point where it passed from sight beyond the trees.

"That's the *car*," Renda said.

Majestyk continued to watch the road, saying nothing until the car appeared again, coming slowly from the other direction.

"All right, let's go."

By the time they reached the road the Jaguar was approaching them and came to an abrupt stop. An attractive young girl with short blond hair and big round sunglasses got out and stood looking at them over the open door.

Majestyk stared, taken by surprise. He hadn't

expected a girl. The possibility had never entered his mind.

"Who's that?"

"That's Wiley," Renda said. He started toward the car and called to the girl, "You got the money?"

"I already gave it to him," the girl said. "God, Frank, you're a mess."

"What do you mean you gave it to him? Come on, for Christ sake, where's the money?"

She was frowning as she raised the sunglasses and placed them on her head. "I was told to stop at the store on the highway and pay the man three dollars and eighty-five cents, and that's what I did. It's the only money I was told to bring."

Renda turned to Majestyk, who was walking toward the Jaguar now, looking at it closely.

"What are you pulling? What kind of shit are you *pulling*! We made a deal—twenty-five grand!"

"It doesn't look like you'd fit in the trunk," Majestyk said. "So I guess maybe you better drive, Frank. Keep your hands on something. Wiley can squeeze in behind the seats." He looked at Renda then. "You can get in by yourself, or I can help you in. Either way."

"I must have missed something," Wiley said. "Is it all right if I ask where we're going?"

Majestyk gave her a pleasant smile. "To jail, honey. Where'd you think?"

*   *   *

Wiley was three years out of Northwestern University, drama school; two years out of Universal City, a little television; one year out of a Las Vegas show-bar, topless; and six months into Frank Renda.

Until recently she had been amazed that life with him could be so—not boring, really—uneventful. Living with a real-life man who killed people had sounded like the trip to end all trips. It turned out to be mostly lying around swimming pools while he talked on the phone. Frank was fun to watch. He was a natural actor and didn't know it. He played roles constantly, from cool dude to spoiled child, and looked at himself in the mirror a lot, like almost every actor she had ever known. It was interesting watching him. Still, it was getting to be something of a drag until, four days ago, when she fingered the guy in the bar for him. No, it wasn't exactly a finger job. What she did was sit at the bar, keeping an eye on the guy. When it looked like he was getting ready to pay his check, she got up and walked out of the place, letting Frank know the guy was coming, giving him a minute or so to get ready. She didn't know what Frank had against the guy; she didn't ask him. This was real-life drama. She stood off to the side and watched Frank calmly shoot the guy five times. Wow. From about ten feet away. The guy was a great dier. It was really a show, cinéma vérité. Until the cop came from out of nowhere and jammed his gun into Frank's back. She got out of there, took a cab back to her apartment and waited, the next four days, close to the phone.

More true-life adventure now, scrunched behind the bucket seats of an XK Jag, driving down a back-country road, her handcuffed boyfriend with both hands on the top arc of the steering wheel, and a solemn-faced, farmer-looking guy staring at him, watching every move he made.

"Left when you get to the blacktop," Majestyk said. "That'll take us to the highway."

Renda braked. As he began to turn onto the county road he lost his grip and had to grab the steering wheel and crank it hard to keep from going into the ditch. Wiley was thrown hard against the back of Majestyk's seat. He glanced around as she straightened up, holding onto the seat.

"Hey, are you trying to put me through the windshield?"

Renda's eyes raised to the rearview mirror and the reflection of Wiley's face. Their eyes met briefly before he shifted his gaze to the road again. Perhaps a minute passed before he glanced at Majestyk.

"All right, you got a new game. What's it cost?"

"Three dollars and eighty-five cents," Majestyk said. "You paid and you're in."

"Come on, cut the bullshit. How much you want?"

"Nothing."

"I explained it as simply as I could," Renda said. "We make a deal or you're dead. I get sent away, you're still dead."

"I've already made a deal."

Renda glanced at him again. "You think the cops can keep you alive? They'd have to live with you the rest of your life. Can you see that? Never knowing when it's going to happen?"

When Majestyk didn't answer, Wiley said, "He's kind of weird, isn't he?"

Renda's eyes raised to the rearview mirror and met Wiley's gaze.

When he looked at the road he saw the curve approaching, waited, started into the curve and braked sharply to reduce his speed. Again Wiley was thrown against Majestyk's seat.

"Hey Frank, take it easy, okay?"

He glanced at her reflection. She was ready.

Coming out of the curve and hitting the straightaway, Renda accelerated to almost seventy, held it for a quarter of a mile, then raised his right foot and mashed it down on the brake pedal.

Wiley already had her hand on the latch to release the backrest of Majestyk's seat. It was free as the car braked suddenly and she threw herself hard against it, her weight and the momentum slamming Majestyk into the dashboard.

"Frank, under the seat!" She screamed it.

"Get it, for Christ sake!"

Renda was accelerating with his left foot, bringing his right foot up and over the transmission hump to kick viciously at Majestyk, jammed between the seat and the dashboard, as Wiley reached beneath the driver's seat, groped frantically, and came up with a Colt .45 automatic in her left hand.

"Shoot him! Shoot the son of a bitch, will you!"

"I don't know how!"

"Pull the fucking trigger!"

Majestyk pushed against the seat back, lunging at Wiley. Renda hit the brakes again, bouncing Majestyk off the dashboard. But he was able to push off from it, twisting around enough to get a hand on the girl's arm just as she fired and the automatic exploded less than a foot from his head.

Renda was kicking at him again. "Christ, shoot him!"

He kicked at Majestyk's ribs, got his heel in hard a couple of times, kicked again and this time his heel hit Majestyk's belt buckle, slipped off and hit the door handle as Wiley pulled her arm free and put the automatic in Majestyk's face. The door opened and she saw him going out, fired, saw his expression and fired twice again, saw the window of the swung-open door shatter, but he was gone, out of the car, and she knew she hadn't hit him.

The XK Jag was two hundred feet up the road before its brake lights flashed on. The car made a tight turn, backed up on the narrow blacktop, and turned again to come back this way.

Majestyk heard the sound of the engine. He was lying facedown on the shoulder of the road, propped on his elbows, dazed, staring at gravel and feeling it cutting into the palms of his hands. His vision was blurred and when he wiped his eyes, he saw blood on the back of his hand. He heard the engine sound louder, winding up, coming toward him. When he raised his head he saw the headlights and the grille, low to the ground, the nose swinging toward the gravel shoulder, coming directly at him.

With all of his strength he threw himself to the side, rolling into the ditch, as the Jag swept past. A moment later he heard the tires squealing on the blacktop and knew he had to get out of here, pushing himself up now, out of the weeds, climbing the bank away from the road and ducking through the wire fence, as the Jag made its tight turn and came back and this time stopped.

Majestyk was running across the open scrub, weaving through the dusty brush clumps, by the time Renda got out of the car and began firing at him with the automatic, both hands extended in the handcuffs. Majestyk kept running. Renda jumped across the ditch, got to the fence, and laid the .45 on the top of a post, aimed, and squeezed the trigger three times, but the figure out in the scrub was too small now and it would have to be a lucky shot to bring him down. He fired once more and the automatic clicked empty.

Seventy, eighty yards away, Majestyk finally came to a stop, worn out, getting his breath. He turned to look at the man standing by the fence post and, for a while, they stared at one another, each knowing who the other man was and what he felt and not having to say anything. Renda crossed the ditch to the Jag and Majestyk watched it drive away.

It seemed easier to get out of jail than it was to get back in.

He got a ride in a feed truck as far as Junction, after walking a couple of miles, then sitting down to rest and waiting almost an hour in the sun. When the driver asked what'd happened to him he said he'd blown a tire and gone off the road and was thrown out when his pickup went into the ditch. The driver said he was lucky he wasn't killed and Majestyk agreed.

At Junction he went into the Enco station and asked the attendant, the one named Gil, for the key to the Men's Room. The attendant gave it to him without saying anything, though he had a little smile on his face looking at Majestyk's dirty, beat-up condition. In the Men's Room he saw what a mess he was: blood and dirt caked on his face, his shirt torn up the back, his hands raw-looking with imbedded gravel.

It was four-thirty that afternoon when he walked into the Edna Post of the County Sheriff's Department and asked the deputy behind the desk if Lieutenant McAllen was around. The deputy, ignoring his face, asked him what it was he wanted to see the lieutenant about.

"I want to go to jail," Majestyk said.

He waited on the bench thinking, Christ, trying to get back in. He was still sitting on the bench twenty minutes later when McAllen walked up to him and stood there, not saying anything.

"I had him," Majestyk said.

"Did you?"

"I guess you want to hear what happened."

"I think I can see," McAllen said.

6

GETTING RENDA to Mexico was no problem. A young guy who brought reefer in two or three times a month flew him down in his Cessna, landing on a desert airstrip not far from Hermosillo. Renda spent two nights in a motel while the rest of it was being worked out. On the morning of the third day an Olds 98 with California plates and a house trailer attached—with Eugene Lundy behind the wheel and Wiley curled on the backseat reading a current bestselling novel—pulled up in front of the motel. Renda, wearing work clothes and a week's growth of beard, walked out of his room and got in the trailer. The Olds took off and didn't stop again until they were on the coast road south of Guaymas and Lundy thought maybe Frank would want to get out and stretch his legs, exercise a little, breathe in the salt air, and throw a couple of stones at the Gulf of California. Wiley said to him, "You don't know Frank very well, do you?"

He didn't come out of the trailer or bother to look up when the door opened. He was sitting in back on one of the bunks, smoking a cigarette.

Wiley said, "Hey, do you love it? I think it's great."

Behind her, Lundy said, "Air-conditioned, you got plenty of vodka, scotch, steaks, and beer in the ice box and"—he took an envelope out of his pocket and handed it to Renda—"twenty-five hundred cigarette money."

Wiley was opening cabinets and doors. "There's a shower in the john. Even a magazine rack."

"Tonight we'll be in Mazatlan," Lundy said. "We can stay there or go on down to Acapulco, it's up to you."

Renda looked up at him. "Regular vacation. You having a nice time?"

"Listen, I think I could use a rest. That stunt, hitting the fucking bus, that took some years off me."

Renda watched him turn to the refrigerator and take out a can of beer.

"Where is he?"

"You want one?"

"I said where is he!"

Lundy, about to pop open the can, looked over at Renda. "The guy? He turned himself in. Last I heard they're still holding him at Edna."

Wiley came in to stretch out on the opposite

bunk. "Kind of tight fit, but all the comforts of home."

"We're not at home," Renda said. "He is."

"He's in jail, Frank." Wiley's tone was soft, approaching him carefully. "You're free. We can go anywhere you want."

"There's only one thing I want," Renda said. "Him."

Lundy opened the can and took a swig. "He gets out, we can have somebody take care of that."

Renda shook his head. "Not somebody. I said *I* want him. I want him to see it and know it's me. Put the gun in his stomach and look at him. Not say anything, just look at him and make sure he understands."

"You still have to wait," Lundy said.

Renda didn't say anything. He was still picturing it, putting the gun in the melon grower's stomach.

"All right, let me ask you," Lundy said. "What do you do, walk in the jail, ask them for a visitor's pass? How do you get close to the guy?"

"You get him out of jail."

"You get him out. How?"

"Find the guy he hit," Renda said. "Tell him to drop the complaint. It was all a mistake, a misunderstanding."

"What if the guy doesn't want to drop it?"

"Jesus, I said *tell* him, not ask him."

"Maybe pay him something?"

"That's up to you. See what it takes."

"You mean you want me to do it? Go back there?"

"I'm talking to you, aren't I?"

"I just wanted to be sure."

"You're going to go back and set it up," Renda said. "Find the guy made the complaint and get that done. Get some people if you see we need them. Call me, I come up. We go in and get out fast. No bullshit screwing around. Arrange it, I walk up to him, and it's done."

Lundy took a sip of beer, getting the right words ready in his mind. "I keep thinking though, what about the cops? They'll be looking for you, watching your house, the apartment."

"Christ, you think I'm going to go home? We'll stay someplace else. Call Harry, tell him to arrange it."

"I mean right now, why take a chance?"

"I told you why."

"I'm not against it," Lundy said. "I'm just thinking, we're this far. Why change your mind all of a sudden?"

"I didn't change it. I hadn't made it up yet. But the more I think about it—I know it's what I'm going to do."

"I was going to lie on the beach," Wiley said, "and read my book."

Lundy waited a moment. "You know, Frank, there's a lot of guys'd do it. I mean guys the cops aren't waiting to flag."

Renda said, "Hey, Gene, one more time. I said I want him. I never wanted anybody so bad and I'm going to do it strictly as a favor to myself. You understand? Am I getting through to you? *I'm* going to do it, not somebody else. Before I take any trips or lay on any beach I'm going to walk up to that melon grower son of a bitch, I'm going to look him in the eyes, and I'm going to kill him."

Harold Ritchie was a pallbearer at his partner's funeral. Bob Almont, good guy to ride with in a squad car, and god*damn* he'd miss him. Shot down in the street by some creepy son of a bitch. Ritchie hoped it was the one he'd shot coming out of the station wagon. He went to Bob Almont's house after the funeral, with Bob's close friends and a few relatives that'd come from Oklahoma. They sat around drinking coffee and picking at the casserole dishes some neighbors had brought over, while Evelyn Almont stayed in the kitchen most of the time or sat with her two little tiny kids who didn't know what the hell was going on. After a couple of hours of watching that, it was a relief to get back to the post.

The deputy at the counter tore off a teletype

sheet and handed it to him. "What you asked for. Just come in."

He read it as he walked over to Lieutenant McAllen's office, knocked twice, and walked in. McAllen was sitting at his desk.

"You're right," Ritchie said, "Phoenix had a sheet on him. Robert L. Kopas, a.k.a. Bobby Kopas, Bobby Curtis. Two arrests, B and E, and extortion. One conviction. Served two years in Florence."

"I could feel it," McAllen said. "The guy's up to something."

"Changed his mind and dropped the charge. The way I read it," Ritchie said, "he's decided it'd be more fun to get back at the guy himself."

"Maybe. But is he smart enough? Or dumb enough to try it? However you want to look at it." McAllen paused. "Or did somebody put him up to it?"

Ritchie was nodding. "That's a thought."

"Yes, it is, isn't it?" McAllen said. "You got any more on Majestyk?"

"On my desk. I'll be right back." Ritchie went out and returned within the minute with an open file folder in his hands, looking at it.

"Not much. He lived in California most of his life. High school education. Truck driver, farm laborer. Owned his own place till he went to Folsom on the assault conviction. Here's something. In the army three years, a Ranger instructor at Fort Benning."

McAllen raised his eyebrows. "An instructor."

"Combat adviser in Laos before that," Ritchie went on. "Captured by the Pathet Lao, escaped and brought three enemy prisoners with him. Got a Silver Star." Looking up at McAllen he said, "Man doesn't fool, does he?"

"Well, he's a different cut than what we usually get."

"Doesn't seem afraid to take chances."

"Doesn't appear to." McAllen was thoughtful a moment. "Let's talk to him and find out."

He said to Majestyk, "You look better than the last time I saw you."

"Thank you, but I'd just as soon wear my own clothes." He was dressed in jail denims with white stripes down the sides of the pants. The scrapes and cuts on his face were healing and he was clean-shaven. "What I'd like to know which nobody'll tell me, is when I'm going to court."

"Why don't you have a seat?" McAllen said.

"I've been sitting for four days."

"So you're used to it," McAllen said. "Sit down."

He watched Majestyk take the chair then picked

up a pack of cigarettes and matches and leaned over to hand them across the desk.

"Have a smoke."

As Majestyk lighted a cigarette, McAllen said, "I guess what you want most is to get out of here."

He waited, but Majestyk, looking at him, said nothing. "Well, I think it might be arranged."

Majestyk continued to wait, not giving McAllen any help.

"The guy you hit, Bobby Kopas?" McAllen said finally. "He dropped the charge against you."

When Majestyk still waited, McAllen said, "You hear what I said?"

"Why'd he do that?"

"He said he thought it over. It wasn't important enough for him to waste a lot of time in court. You think that's the reason?"

"I met him once," Majestyk said. "I can't say I know him or what's in his head."

"He's got a record. Extortion, breaking and entering. Does that tell you anything?"

"You say it, I believe it."

"I'm saying he could have a reason of his own to see you walking around free."

"Well, whatever his reason is, I'll go along with it," Majestyk said. "If it means getting my crop in."

"You can stay if you want," McAllen said.

"Why would I want to?"

"Because Frank Renda's also walking around free."

Majestyk saw him waiting for his reaction and he said, "Why don't you just tell me what you're going to anyway, without all the suspense."

McAllen looked over at Ritchie and back again. He said, "The eyeball witness who saw Frank Renda commit murder was an off-duty police officer."

"I heard that."

"He was a member of this department."

Majestyk waited.

"He was killed during Renda's escape. Shot dead. So there's no witness. The gun Renda used— is alleged to have used—can't be traced to him. That means there's no case."

"If you want him so bad," Majestyk said, "why don't you arrest him for the escape?"

"Because there's no way to tie him in with the attempt. His lawyer made that clear and the prosecutor had to agree. Technically—and tell me how you like this?—he was kidnapped. We can stick you with that if we want. Or let you go. Or, we can hold you in protective custody."

"Protective custody against what?"

"Frank Renda. What do you think he's going to do when he finds out you're on the street?"

"I don't know. What?"

"He might've already found out. Though right now we don't know where he is or what he's doing."

Majestyk took a drag on the cigarette and let the smoke out slowly. "Are you trying to tell me my life's in danger?"

"You should know him by now. What do you think?"

"Why would he risk getting arrested again? I mean just to get me."

"Because it's his business. Now you've given him a personal reason to kill," McAllen said. "And I can't think of anything that would stop him trying."

"You're that sure."

"He might even think it would be easy. Get careless again, like he did the last time."

"Something's finally starting to get through," Majestyk said. "You'll let me go if I'll sit home and act as your bait."

"Something like that."

"Maybe even you'd like him to shoot me, so you can get him for murder."

"That entered my mind," McAllen said, "but we'll settle for attempted."

"Attempted, huh? And if he pulls it off, you try something else then?"

"I believe you're the guy who wanted to make a

deal," McAllen said, "so you could get your melons picked. All right, go pick them."

"And where'll you be?"

"We'll be around."

"He could send somebody else."

"He could." McAllen nodded. "Or he could wait a few months, or a year. Shoot you some night while you're sleeping. Or wire your truck with dynamite. One morning you get in and turn the key—" McAllen paused. "No, you're right, we don't know for certain he'll try for you himself, just as we can't guarantee we'll be able to stop him if he does. It's a chancy situation any way you look at it. But remember, you got yourself into it. So, as things stand, it's the best offer I can make."

"Well then"—Majestyk got up from the chair, stubbing out the cigarette—"I guess there's no reason for me to hang around, is there?"

7

IT WAS STILL COOL at 6:00 A.M., the vines were wet and darkened the pants legs of the pickers as they worked along the rows with their burlap sacks. Somebody said it was insecticide, the wetness, but most of them knew the fields had not been sprayed in several days and that moisture had settled during the night. Their pants and the vines would be hot and dusty dry within an hour. The sun, which they would have all day, faced them from the eastern boundary of the fields, above a tangle of willows that lined an arroyo five miles away. The sun seemed that close to them.

Larry Mendoza stood by the pickup truck counting the stooped, round figures in the rows. He had counted them before, but he counted them again and got the same number. Twelve, including Nancy Chavez and the ones from Yuma—thank God for them. But he wasn't going to get any crop in with twelve people. Some of them had never picked before—like the two Anglo kids he'd been able to get because nobody else wanted them.

He saw one of them stretching in his white T-shirt, rolling his shoulders to work the ache out of his back, and Mendoza yelled at him, "Hey, how you going to pick melons standing up!"

He crossed the ditch and went out into the field, toward the white T-shirt that said *Bronco Athletic Dept.* and had a small numeral on it, 22, in a square.

"I was seeing how much I had in the sack," the white Anglo kid said.

"Fill it," Larry Mendoza told him. "That's how much you put in. Then you stand up."

"I'm getting used to it already."

A colored guy he had hired that morning, who was working the next row, was watching them. Mendoza said to him, "You need something? You want some help or something?"

The colored guy didn't answer; he turned and stooped over and went back to work. At least the colored guy had picked before, not melons, but he had picked and knew what he was doing. The Anglo kid, with his muscular arms and shoulders and cut-off pants and tennis shoes—like he was out here on his vacation—couldn't pick his nose.

"This one"—Mendoza took a honeydew from the Anglo kid's sack—"it's not ready. Remember I told you, you pick the *ripe ones*. You loosen the other ones in the dirt. You don't turn them so the sun hits the underneath, you just loosen them."

"That's what I been doing," the Anglo kid said.

"The ones aren't ready, we come back for later on."

"I thought it was ripe." The Anglo kid stooped to lay the melon among the vine leaves.

Larry Mendoza closed his eyes and opened them and adjusted the funneled brim of his straw hat. "You going to put it back on the vine? Tie it on? You pick it, it stays picked. You got to keep it then. You understand?"

"Sure," the Anglo kid said.

Sure. How do you find them? Mendoza asked himself, turning from the kid who might last the day but would never be back tomorrow. Walking to the road his gaze stopped on another big-shouldered, blond-haired Bronco from Edna and he yelled at him, "Hey, whitey, where are you, in church? Get off your knees or go home, I get somebody else!" Christ, he wasn't paying them a buck forty an hour to rest. He yelled at the guy again, "You hear me? I'll get somebody else!"

"Like it's easy," Nancy Chavez said. She was going over to the trailer with a full sack of melons hanging from her shoulder. Pretty girl, thin but strong-looking, with a dark bandana and little pearl earrings.

"I may have to go to Mexico," Mendoza said.

"Christ, nobody wants to work anymore. And some of the ones I got don't know how."

"Teach them," the girl said. "Somebody had to teach you."

"Yeah, when I was eight years old." He went over to the pickup truck and got in. "Now I got to tell Vincent. He don't have enough to worry about."

"Tell him we'll get it done," the girl said. "Somehow."

Majestyk came out through the screen door of his house to wait on the porch. When he saw the pickup coming he walked out to the road. Larry Mendoza moved over and Majestyk got in behind the wheel.

"How'd you sleep?"

"Too long."

"Man, you need it."

Majestyk swung the pickup around in a tight turn. When they were heading back toward the field that was being worked, on their right now, Mendoza said, "I try again this morning, same thing. Nobody wants to work for us. I talk to Julio Tamaz, some of the others. What's going on? What is this shit? Julio says man, I don't have a crew for you, that's all."

"He can get all he wants," Majestyk said.

"I know it. He turn some away, says they're no good. I hire them and find out he's right."

As they approached the trailer, standing by itself on the side of the road, Mendoza saw the girl with the dark bandana and pearl earrings coming out of the field again with a sack of melons. He glanced at Majestyk and saw him watching her.

"That one," Mendoza said, "Nancy Chavez. She wasn't here, we wouldn't have any good workers at all. She got some more friends drove over from Yuma. She picks better than two men. But we got to have a full crew, soon, or we never get it done."

Mendoza got out by the trailer. He slammed the door and said through the window, "I hope you have better luck than me."

"Least I'll find out what's going on," Majestyk said. He could see the girl by the trailer, unloading her melon sack. That was something, she was still here. She didn't know him or owe him anything, but she was still here.

Harold Ritchie was leaning over the fender of the State Highway Department pickup truck, holding a pair of binoculars to his eyes. He was looking across the highway and across a section of melon field to where the dust column was following Majestyk's yellow truck all the way up the side road.

"It could be him this time," Ritchie said. "Hang on."

He was speaking to another deputy who was sitting inside a tool shed by a police-frequency two-way radio. It was hotter than hell inside and the door was open so he could get some air. The shed hadn't been built for people to sit in, but it was the best they could do. Besides the shed, there was a mobile generator, a tar pot, some grading equipment, a pile of gravel, a portable toilet that looked like a rounded phone booth without windows, wooden barricades and lanterns and a sign that said ROAD CONSTRUCTION 500 FT., though nothing was going on. The only ones here were Ritchie and the deputy operating the radio, both of them in work clothes.

"Yeah, it's him," Ritchie said now, lowering the glasses and watching Majestyk's pickup come out of the side road without stopping and swing onto the highway. "Jesus Christ, I could arrest him for that," Ritchie said. "Tell them he just drove out in his truck, yellow four-wheel-drive pickup, heading toward Edna. I'm getting on him right now."

Ritchie slid behind the wheel of the State Highway Department truck and took off after him.

Majestyk parked across the highway from the blue school bus and the stake truck and the old junk cars the migrants would return to later in the day. In the stillness he could hear the jukebox out on the street. Tammy Wynette, with a twangy Nashville backup, telling about some boy she loved who was in love with somebody else.

Majestyk followed the sound of the music to the café-bar and had the screen door open when the State Highway Department truck slowed down at the Junction intersection and came coasting by. He gave the truck a little wave before he went inside.

A waitress was serving Julio Tamaz and another Chicano labor contractor their breakfast. They were sitting at a table, the only customers in the place. Another woman, wearing a stained white apron, was sweeping the floor, moving chairs around, banging them against the formica tables. The two men didn't look up as Majestyk approached them. They were busy with the salt and pepper and pouring sugar and cream. Julio was dousing his fried eggs dark brown with Lea & Perrins.

"Julio?"

He looked up then, with a surprised expression he had prepared as Majestyk walked over.

"Hey, Vincent. They let you out, huh? Good."

Majestyk pulled a chair out but didn't sit down. He stood with his hand on it, as though he had changed his mind.

"How come I can't hire a crew?"

"Man, you been away, in jail."

"Larry Mendoza hasn't. Last two mornings you turned him down. How come?"

"It's the time of the year. I got too much business." He poked at the eggs with his fork, yellow appearing, mixing with the brown. "Other people need crews too. They ask me first."

"All right," Majestyk said, "I'm asking you right now for thirty people tomorrow morning. Buck forty."

Julio kept busy with his eggs and didn't look up. "I got crews signed more than a week. Vincent, you too late, that's all."

Majestyk watched him begin to eat his eggs before turning his attention to the other man at the table. He was already finishing, wiping the yolk from his plate with a piece of toast.

"How about you?" Majestyk said. "You get me a crew?"

"Me?" With the same helpless tone as Julio's. "Maybe in ten days," the labor contractor said. "I can't promise you nothing right now."

"In ten days my crop will be ruined."

"Like Julio says, other people ask first. We can't help that."

"What is this, stick-up time? You want more money? What?"

"It's not money, Vincent." Julio's tone was sad as

well as helpless. "How can we get you people if we don't have any?"

Majestyk pulled the chair out a little farther. This time he sat down and leaned over the edge of the table on his arms.

He said quietly, "Julio, what's going on?"

"I tole you. I got too much work."

"You'd drive to Mexico if you had to. Come on, somebody pay you, threaten you? What?"

"Listen," Julio said, intently now, his voice lower, "I got to work for a living and I can't do it in no goddamn hospital. You understand?"

"I'm beginning to. You could help me though."

"I'm not going to say any more. Man, I've said enough."

Majestyk stared at him a moment. Finally he said, "Okay," got up and walked away from the table.

Julio called after him, "Vincent, next season, uh?"

The contractor at the table with him, eating his piece of toast, said, "If he's still around."

Coming out of the place into the sunlight he was aware of the State Highway Department truck parked across the street and the deputy sitting in the cab, watching him. Tell him you're going back home, Majestyk was thinking. Put his mind at ease. He started for the street, through the space between the back of the school bus and the stake truck, when the voice stopped him.

"You looking for a crew?"

He saw Bobby Kopas then, leaning against a car with his arms folded, a familiar pose, a tight lavender shirt; sunglasses and bandit moustache hiding a thin, bony face. The car, an Olds 98, was at the curb in front of the school bus. Someone else was inside, a big-shouldered man, behind the wheel.

"You want pickers, maybe I can get you some wine heads," Kopas said. He straightened, unfolding his arms, as Majestyk walked over to him. "You touch me, man, you're back in jail by lunchtime."

Majestyk stared at him, standing there close enough to touch. All he had to do was grab the front of that pretty shirt and belt him. It would be easy and it would be pure pleasure. But the deputy was across the street and Majestyk didn't have to look over to know he was watching them. He wondered if Kopas knew the man in the State Highway Department truck was a cop.

"You dropped the complaint," Majestyk said. "Why? You want to try and pay me back yourself?"

"I do you a favor—Jesus, after you like to broke my nose, you think I'm pulling something." Kopas gave him the hint of a grin. "Man, I'm being a good neighbor, that's all."

"What'd you say to Julio Tamaz and the other contractors? You pay them off or threaten them? How'd you work it?"

The little grin was still there. "Man, I hope nobody's telling stories on me, giving me a bad name."

"They didn't say it was you. I'm saying it."

"Why would I do a thing like that?"

"So I'll lose my crop."

"I think you must be a little mixed up," Kopas said. "Don't know where your head's at. Here you are standing in deep shit and you're worried about a little dinky melon crop."

"You've been talking to somebody," Majestyk said.

"Who's that?" Kopas said, giving him the grin.

"I can fix it you'd have a hard time smiling again."

Kopas tensed and the grin vanished. "Listen, I'm not kidding. You even make a fist, man, you're back in jail."

"Are you working for him?"

"Who's that?"

"He get you to drop the complaint?"

"I think I'm tired of talking to you," Kopas said. He moved to the car door and opened it, then looked back at Majestyk.

"I'll tell you one thing though. Somebody's going to set your ass on fire. And I'm going to be there to see it."

The Olds started off as Kopas got in and slammed the door.

Majestyk caught a glimpse of the driver's profile— looking at Kopas, saying something—and for a moment he thought he knew the man or had seen him before. But the car was moving away and it was too late to get another look at him and be sure. Big shoulders, curly hair. Maybe he was one of the guys who had been with Kopas a week ago, the day it began. Or a different one. The car was different.

What difference did it make? He had enough people to think about without bringing in new ones. Faces to remember. Frank Renda's. Telling him he was going to kill him. Now Kopas and Renda. The man had already started to make his move. He didn't waste time. He found Kopas and hired him. That was plain enough. Now they were beginning to play a game with him. Let him know they were coming. Give him something to keep him awake nights. He thought of telling the deputy in the State Highway Department truck. Get him after them, quick, before they turned off the highway somewhere. Maybe they would lead him to Renda.

But Renda didn't have any reason to hide. He was free.

And what does the cop do, arrest them? For what?

No, whatever's going to happen is going to happen, Majestyk thought. So go home and pick your melons.

8

"**I'M NOT SHITTIN' YOU,**" Kopas said. "I was thinking of dropping the complaint anyway, so I could take care of the son of a bitch myself."

Eugene Lundy wasn't listening to him. He was staring straight ahead, over the hood of the Olds 98, at the vacant land of dust-green mesquite and sun glare and bugs rising with the airstream and exploding in yellow bursts against the windshield. Like somebody was spitting them there.

"Load up the pump gun and wait for him," Kopas said. "Or stick it in his window some night. See him sittin' on the toilet. *Bam*. Scatter the motherfucker all over the room."

Lundy was counting the bug stains, more than a dozen of the yellow ones: some kind of bug flying along having a nice time and the next thing sucked into the wind, coming up fast over the hood and wiped out, the bug not knowing what in the name of Christ happened to him. Maybe they had been butterflies. Seeing the bugs suddenly, there wasn't time to tell what they were.

"I got to piss," Kopas said.

Lundy looked at the speedometer and up again. He was holding between seventy and seventy-five down the country road that rose and dropped through the desert, seeing no other cars, no people, not even signs.

"Man, I'm in pain," Kopas said. "All you got to do is stop the car."

"We're almost there," Lundy said. "I'm not going to stop twice."

"How long you think it's going to take me, an hour? All I want to do is take a piss."

"Hold it," Lundy said.

Maybe they were all different kinds of bugs, but all bugs were yellow inside. Like all people were red inside. Maybe. Lundy had never thought about it before. His gaze held on the stained windshield as he waited for a bug to come up over the hood.

He felt so good his eyes were watering, and kept going like he was never going to stop. Jesus, what a relief. Son of a bitch Lundy made him hold it twenty minutes, refusing to stop the car. He'd finally pleaded with him. Christ, just slow down, he'd piss out the window, but the son of a bitch wouldn't even do that. A very cold son of a bitch who didn't say much, sitting on two pieces under his seat, a Colt .45 automatic and a big fucking Colt .44 mag. He had asked the guy if he had been in on the bus job and the guy had looked at him and said, "The bus job. Is that what you call it?" And that was all he'd said.

Bobby Kopas zipped up his fly and walked around to the front of the Olds where Lundy was standing, squinting up at the sky.

"Hurry up and wait," Kopas said. "I never seen a plane come in on time in my life. Not even the airlines, not once I ever went out to the airport. Everybody sitting around waiting. Go in the cocktail lounge you're smashed by the time the fucking plane arrives. You ever seen a plane come in on time?"

Staring at the sky and the flat strip of desert beyond the road, Lundy said, "Why don't you shut your mouth for a while?"

Christ, you couldn't even talk to the guy. Kopas moved around with his hands in his pockets, kicking a few stones, looking around for some shade, which there wasn't a bit of anywhere, squinting in the hot glare, squinting even with his wraparound sunglasses on. The glasses made him sweat and he had to keep wiping his eyes. Lundy stood there not moving, like the heat didn't bother him at all. Big, heavy son of a bitch who should've been lathered with sweat by now, like a horse.

They heard the plane before they saw it, the far-away droning sound, then a dot in the sky coming in low, the sun flashing on its windshield. The Cessna passed over them at about a hundred feet. As it banked, descending, coming around in a wide circle, Lundy finally spoke. He said, "Wait here," and walked out into the desert.

Kopas was excited now. He wanted to appear cool and make a good impression. He put his hands on his hipbones and cocked one leg, pointing the toe of the boot out a little. Like a gunfighter. So the guy was big time. He'd act cool, savvy, show the guy he wasn't all that impressed.

He watched the plane come to a stop about a hundred yards away. Lundy, going out to meet it, was holding up his arm, waving at the plane. Big jerk.

Renda came out first and then the girl—white slacks and a bright green blouse. Even at this distance she looked good. Blond, nice slim figure. Now they were coming this way and Lundy was talking to them, gesturing, probably telling Renda how the murder charge against him had been dropped. Renda wouldn't have known about it, though the pilot might have told him. As the plane started its engine to take off, the prop wash blew sand at them and they hunched their shoulders and turned away from the stinging blast of air. Lundy was talking again. Renda stopped and they all stopped. Renda was saying something.

Then Lundy was talking again. As they came up to the road Kopas heard Lundy say, "You could have rode up here bareass on a white horse, nobody would've stopped you."

"What about the bus thing?" the girl asked him. She was something. Maybe the best-looking girl Bobby Kopas had ever seen.

"There's nothing they can stick you with," Lundy said. "The bus, nothing. They tried to, naturally. There're three cops involved and they don't like that one bit. But what're they going to stick you with? You didn't shoot the cops. You didn't take the bus. The guy did, Majestyk. But they don't even jam him for that. You see what I'm getting at?"

Kopas had never heard Lundy talk so much.

The good-looking girl said, "God, nothing like a little dumb luck."

"Luck, bullshit," Renda said. "Timing. Make it happen. And never run till you see you're being chased."

"With a fast lawyer available at all times," the girl said. She didn't seem to be afraid of him.

"They had to let him go," Renda said. "I could see that right away, the cops coming up with this great idea. Don't stick him with the bus, no, let him go so I'll show up and try for him."

"That's the question," Lundy said. "What're the cops doing?"

"No, the question is what's the guy doing? Is he still sitting for it or what?"

"He's around," Lundy said. "We just saw him."

Kopas stepped out of the way as they approached the Olds. He set a grin on his face and said, "Probably home by now waiting on you, Mr. Renda."

Renda looked at him. Christ, with the coldest look he'd ever gotten from a person. Like he was a thing or wasn't even there. Christ, he'd been arrested, he'd been in the can. He wasn't some lightweight who didn't know what he was doing.

He said, "Mr. Renda? I wonder if I could ask you a favor." Renda was looking at him again. "I know it's your party, but—after you finish the son of a bitch—you mind if I put a couple of slugs in him?"

Renda said to Lundy, "Who's this asshole?"

"Bobby Kopas. Boy Majestyk hit."

"You pay him to drop it?"

"Five hundred."

"Then what's he doing here?"

"He's working for us," Lundy said, "to see nobody works for Majestyk. So there won't be a crowd hanging around there. He knows the guy's place, back roads, ways in and out. I thought he might come in handy."

Kopas thought he could add to that. He said, "I

been watching that Polack melon picker since they
let him out. He doesn't fart that I don't know
about it."

The girl said, probably to Lundy, "Is he for
real?"

Kopas wasn't sure what she meant. He kept his
eyes on Renda, who was staring at him, and tried
not to look away.

"You're telling me you know him pretty well?"
Renda asked.

"I know he's a stuck-up son of a bitch. Got a
two-bit farm and thinks he's a big grower."

"How long's he lived here?"

Kopas grinned. "Not much longer I guess, huh?"

"I ask you a question," Renda said, "you don't
seem to want to answer it."

Jesus, that look again. "Well, I'm not sure how
long exactly he's been here. Couple years, I guess. I
just got into this labor business recently, when I
seen there was money in it."

"Show me where he lives," Renda said.

"Yes sir, any time you say."

"Right now."

"Frank," Lundy said, "your lawyer got the
house, it's all set. Up in the mountains, nobody can
bother you or know you're there. I thought maybe
you'd want to go up to the house first, you know,
take it easy for a while."

Renda said, "Gene, did I come here to take it

easy? I could be home, not at some place in the mountains. But I'm not home."

"I know you're anxious," Lundy began.

"Gene, I want to see the guy's place," Renda said. "I want to see it right now."

The two Anglo kids in the white T-shirts quit at noon and Mendoza paid them off. That left nine. So Majestyk went out in the field and picked melons all the rest of the day with Nancy Chavez and her friends from Yuma. Maybe next year he could stand around and watch, or sit in an office like a big melon grower. Sit on the porch and drink iced tea. That would be nice.

He wasn't used to this. He could feel the soreness in his back, and each time he reached the end of a row it would take him a little longer to straighten up. All day, dirty and sweaty and thirsty—drinking the lukewarm water in the canvas bag. Tomorrow he'd get a tub of ice and some pop, cover it with a piece of burlap. He'd forgotten how difficult and painful stooped labor was. Around 5:30, after eleven hours of it, the pickers began to straggle out of the field and unload their last melon sacks at the trailer parked on the road.

Majestyk was finishing a row, finally, when Nancy Chavez crossed through the vines and came toward him, a full sack hanging from her shoulder.

She said, "I've been watching you. For a grower you're pretty good."

"Lady, I've picked way more'n I've ever grown." He got up with an effort, trying not to show it, and the girl smiled at him. As they moved off toward the trailer, where Mendoza and two of his small sons were emptying the sacks and stacking the melons, Majestyk said, "I meant to ask if you ever sorted."

"All the time. It's what I do best."

"Maybe you could start things going in the packing shed tomorrow. If you'd like to."

"Whatever you say."

"We ever get it done, I'd like to pay everybody something extra."

"You worried we won't take it?"

"I just want you to know I appreciate your staying here and all."

"Don't mention it. You're paying, aren't you?"

"Are the quarters all right? They haven't been used in a while. Couple of years at least."

"They're okay," the girl said. "We've lived in worse."

They were approaching the trailer and he wanted to say something to her before they reached it and Mendoza might hear him.

"You want to have supper with me?"

She turned her head to look at him. "Where, your house? Just the two of us, all alone?"

"We can go down the highway you want. I don't care."

They were at the trailer now. She handed up her sack to Mendoza before looking at Majestyk again.

"For a man needs a job done, where do you get all this free time? You want to pack melons, why don't we start?"

"You mean tonight?"

"Why not?"

"They'd keep working?"

"For money. You make it when you can." She said then, "If you don't want to ask them, I'll do it. We'll eat, then go to the packing shed and work another half shift. All right?"

"Lady," Majestyk said, "you swing that I'll marry you and give you a home."

She seemed to be considering it, her expression serious, solemn, before saying, "How about if I settle for a cold beer after work?"

"All you want."

"Maybe a couple."

She gave him a nice look and walked away, up the road toward the migrant quarters. Both Majestyk and Mendoza, on the trailer, stood watching her.

Mendoza said, "You like a piece of that, huh?" He looked down at Majestyk's deadpan expression and added quickly, "Hey, I don't mean nothing. Take it easy."

Majestyk handed him his sack. "You hear what she said? They'll start packing tonight."

Mendoza emptied the sack and came down off the trailer while his sons stacked the melons. "You must live right," he said. "Or maybe it's time you had some good luck for a change." He nodded toward the migrant quarters, fishing a cigarette out of his shirt pocket. "Those people, they're twice as good as what Julio brings up. They work hard because they like you. They don't want to see you lose a crop."

"I don't know," Majestyk said. "Maybe we can do it."

"We'll do it, Vincent. Don't get anybody else mad at you, we'll do it."

"We're coming to it now," Kopas said, over his shoulder. "On the right there. That's his packing shed."

Renda and Wiley were in the back seat. Lundy was driving, slowing down now as they approached the yellow building with MAJESTYK BRAND MELONS painted on the side.

"See," Kopas said. "Puts his name up as big as he can get it. Down the end of that road we're coming to the house. Way down, where you see the trees."

Renda was studying the road, then hunching forward to look across the field at the road, at the trailer and the figures in the road and the three old cars parked in front of the migrant living quarters.

He sat back again. "You said nobody was working for him."

"No crews," Kopas said. "He picked up a few migrants, that's all."

"They're people, aren't they?"

"Some claim they are. I don't." Christ, he knew right away he shouldn't have said it. It slipped out, talking smart again and not answering his question direct. He waited, looking straight ahead, knowing it was coming. But Renda didn't say anything for a moment, not until they were passing the sign that said ROAD CONSTRUCTION 500 FT., passing the barricades and equipment, the portable toilet and the State Highway Department pickup truck.

He said then, "Go up to the next road and turn around."

Lundy's eyes raised to the rearview mirror. "You want another look at his layout? That's all there is, what you saw."

"Gene," Renda said, "turn the fucking car around."

They had to go up about a mile to do it. Coming back, approaching the road repair site again, Renda said, "How long's that been there?"

Kopas wasn't sure what he meant at first and had to twist around to see where he was looking.

"That road stuff? I don't know, a few days."

"How long!" Renda's voice drilled into the back of his head and Kopas kept staring at the barricades and equipment as they approached, trying to remember, trying to recall quickly how many days.

"They been there as long as I been watching his place. I'm sure of that."

Now they were even with the site, going past it. Kopas was looking out the side window and saw the guy in khaki work clothes getting into the pickup truck. It was a close look at a face he'd seen somewhere before, but only a quick glimpse, and he was turning to look back when Renda's voice hit him in the head again.

"It's *cops*! Jesus, don't you know a cop when you see one!"

Kopas was turned, trying to see the guy, but it was too late. Looking past Renda, trying not to meet his eyes, he said, "You sure? I thought if there was any cops around I'd recognize them."

And he remembered as he said it and turned back around to stare at the windshield. Christ yes, the guy was a deputy. He'd seen him in Edna, at the station. He'd seen him in the pickup earlier today, across the street, when he was talking to Majestyk.

Kopas gave himself a little time, trying to relax and sound natural, before he said, "Well, I figure after a while they get tired waiting, they'll pick up and leave."

Nobody said anything.

"Then we can run off those Mexicans he's got. No sweat to that."

There was a silence again before Renda said, "Pull over."

Lundy looked up. "What?"

"Pull over, for Christ sake, and stop the car."

Lundy braked, bringing the Olds to a gradual stop on the shoulder of the road. They sat in silence, waiting for Renda.

"Hey, asshole. Get out of the car."

"Me?"

Kopas turned enough to look over his shoulder. Renda was staring the way he had stared before—as if not even seeing him—and he knew the man wasn't going to say anything.

"What did you want me to do?"

"Get out," Lundy said. "That's all you have to do."

Kopas grinned. "Is this a joke or something?"

Nobody was laughing. The girl had a book open and was reading, not even paying any attention.

Kopas said to Lundy, "I mean I left my car in Edna, where you picked me up. That's a six-mile hike just back to Junction."

Lundy didn't say anything.

Kopas waited another moment before he got out and turned to the car to close the door. He saw the window next to Renda lower without a sound.

"Come here," Renda said.

Kopas hunched over to look in the window. The girl was still reading the book.

"You hear me all right?"

"Yes, sir, fine."

"The way you come on," Renda said, "I don't like it. I don't know you a half hour you start talking shit out the side of your mouth. I say I don't want anybody working for him, he's got a dozen people living there. The cops set up a fucking grandstand to watch the show, you don't know they're cops. What I'm saying, I don't see you're doing me a lot of good."

"Mr. Renda, I been watching, seeing he doesn't run off."

"I'll tell you what," Renda said. "You go home, maybe we'll see you, maybe not. But listen, if it happens don't ever talk shit to me again, okay? Don't ever tell me what I'm going to do."

"I sure didn't mean anything like that, Mr. Renda."

But that was the end of it and he knew it. The window went up, the Olds drove off and Bobby Kopas was left standing there, six miles from Edna, feeling like a dumb shit who'd blown his chance.

9

RENDA'S LAWYER was a senior partner in a firm that represented a number of businessmen and business organizations who shared related or complementary interests. Renda's lawyer looked out for his clients, helping them any way he could, and liked to see them help one another, too. For example, he had a client, a mortgage broker, who was spending twelve months in the Federal Penitentiary at Lewisburg for willfully conspiring to defraud the United States government. All right, the mortgage broker had a hunting lodge-weekend funhouse up in the mountains that he wasn't using. Frank Renda, he was informed, wanted some solitude, a place to rest where no one would bother him. So Renda's lawyer arranged for Frank to lease the place from the mortgage broker for only six hundred dollars a week.

That was all right with the lawyer, Frank wanting a place in the mountains. But it wasn't all right if he was going to sit up there on his ass worrying about a 160-acre melon grower when he should be attending to his commercial affairs: his restaurant linen service, his laundry and dry cleaning supply company, his modeling service, and his string of massage parlors. That's where the money was to be made; not in shooting people.

The lawyer knew Frank Renda very well—his moods, his inclinations—so he knew it was sometimes hard to get through to him, once he had made up his mind. He began calling Frank at the mortgage broker's hunting lodge an hour after the Cessna was scheduled to drop him in the desert. There was no answer at the place until late afternoon, and then he had to wait another ten minutes before Renda came to the phone.

Wiley handed it to him, the phone and a scotch, and went over to a bearskin couch where her reading glasses and her novel were waiting.

Renda stood looking around the room, at the Navajo blankets and mounted heads of antelope and mule deer, the shellacked beams and big wagon-wheel chandelier, antique guns and branding irons. Christ, western shit all over the place. He had never met the mortgage broker friend of his lawyer, but he could picture the guy now: little Jew-boy with a cowboy hat, string tie and high-heeled boots, and horn-rimmed glasses and a big fucking cigar.

He said into the phone, "Yeah."

His lawyer's calm, unhurried voice came on. "How are you, Frank? How was the trip?"

"Great, and the weather's great if it doesn't rain or snow. Come on, Harry, what do you want?"

"You like the place all right?"

"It looks like a fucking dude ranch."

"I called a few times this afternoon." The tone was still calm, unhurried. "Where've you been?"

"On the can," Renda said. "I come here to get away, I'm in the fucking place ten minutes and the phone starts ringing."

"I'm not going to bother you," the lawyer said. "I want to let you know how the situation stands."

"I thought I was clear."

"You are at the moment. Technically you're free on a five-thousand-dollar bond, pending your appearance at an investigation in ten days. It's a formality, something to inconvenience us. Though there is the possibility they'll try to dream up a lesser charge."

"No they won't," Renda said. "They don't want to touch me unless it's for the big one."

"I'm glad you understand that," the lawyer said. "So you know this is not the time to do anything"— he paused—"that would bring you under suspicion. Frank, they want you very badly."

"What else is new?"

"You must also have figured out why they released the melon grower."

Renda didn't say anything.

"All right," the lawyer said, "then let me mention that you have business matters that need your attention."

"Anything I was doing can wait."

"And you have business associates," the lawyer went on, "who may not feel like waiting. It's been my experience that the general reaction is one of impatience with anyone who puts his personal affairs ahead of the . . . common good, if you will."

"I've got something to do," Renda said. "I think they understand that. If they don't, tough shit."

"All right, you're saying you're going to do what you want," the lawyer said. "I want it on record that I'm advising you to wait—"

"You got your machine on?"

"Getting every word. As I was saying, I want it on record that I'm advising you to wait. I'm suggesting that any dealings you might have with the melon grower would be extremely ill-timed."

"Harry," Renda said, "don't fuck with me, okay? I need you, I'll call you."

He hung up.

Wiley rested her book on her lap and looked over the top of her reading glasses.

"What did he want?"

"The usual shit. Lawyers, they talk and talk, they don't say anything."

"I'll bet he told you not to do anything hasty,"

Wiley said. He didn't answer. She watched him sit
down with his scotch and take a drink, sipping it,
thinking about something.

She tried again. "After all, you pay him for his
advice."

He looked over at her. "And you know what I
pay you for. So why don't you shut the fuck up?"

"You don't pay me."

"It's the same thing."

She was starting to annoy him. Not too much
yet, but she was starting. He had dumped a wife
who had bored the shit out of him, talking all the
time, buying clothes and showing them to him, and
now he had a girl who was a college graduate
drama major, very bright, who read dirty books.
Books she thought were dirty. He said to himself,
Where are you? What the fuck are you doing?

Five years ago it had been better, simpler. Get a
name, do a study on the guy, learn his habits, walk
up to him at the right time, and pull the trigger. It
was done. Take a vacation, wait for a call, and
come back. L.A., Vegas, wherever they wanted
him. Now it was business all the time. The boring
meetings, discussions, planning, all the fucking papers to sign and talking on the phone. Phones all
over the place. He used to have one phone. It would
ring, he'd say hello, and a voice would give him the
name. That was it. He didn't even have to say
good-bye. Now he had six phones in his house,

four in the apartment. He took Librium and De-
merol and Maalox and even smoked reefer sometimes, which he had never done before in his life or
trusted anybody who did. A hundred and fifty
grand plus a year to talk on the phone and sign the
papers. He used to take a contract for five grand
and had got as much as ten when it was tricky or
the guy had a name.

That's what he missed. The planning and then
pulling the trigger, being very steady, with no
wasted motions. Then lying around after, drinking
all the scotch he wanted for a while and thinking
about how he'd pulled the trigger. He was good
then. During the last few days he had caught himself wondering if he was still good and would be
good enough to hit the melon grower clean. He
hadn't hit the guy coming out of the bar very clean
and that was probably why it was on his mind. He
hadn't hit anybody in a while and had taken the job
because he missed the action and had talked them
into letting him hit the guy, who wasn't anybody at
all to speak of. But he had been too *up*, too anxious
to pull the trigger and experience the feeling again,
and he hadn't blueprinted the job the way he
should have. Christ, an off-duty cop sitting there
watching. Empty the gun like a fucking cowboy
and not have any left for the cop. Or not looking
around enough beforehand. Not noticing the cop.

Like it was his first time or like his fucking brains were in his socks. They could be wondering about him right now. What's the matter with him? Can't he pull a simple hit anymore?

No, they wouldn't be thinking that. They didn't know enough about it, how you made it work. They'd think it was dumb luck the cop was there and dumb luck the cop was killed and couldn't finger him. So the two canceled each other out and he was okay.

Except somebody had talked to the lawyer and that's why the lawyer had talked to him. It wasn't the lawyer's idea to call—he realized that now without any doubt. The lawyer wouldn't do anything unless he was getting paid to do it or somebody had told him to. Their lawyer, *they*, were telling him not to go after the melon grower. Because they thought he was wasting time or because it might involve them in some way or because they didn't have anything against the guy. The guy had not done anything to the organization. If he had, sure, hit him. They could pay him to do it and he wouldn't think any more about it. That was the difference. He *was* thinking about it and this time they couldn't pay him to hit the guy. He wouldn't take it. That was the thing. He couldn't get the melon grower out of his head he wanted to hit him so bad, and he wasn't sure why. Not because the guy had belted him a couple of times; though that could be reason enough. No, it was the way the guy had looked at him. The way he talked. The way he pulled that cheap cool shit and acted like he couldn't be bought.

How do you explain that to them?

Look, I *want* to hit the guy. I got to. I want him—listen, I never gave a shit about anybody before in my life, anybody I hit. It was never a personal thing before like this one.

Or try this.

Listen, if nobody gives a bunch of shit about this, if you let me hit him, then I'll give you the next one, anybody you want, free.

He said to himself, For Christ sake, you going to ask permission? You want the guy, do it.

And he yelled, "Gene."

Wiley looked up from her book.

Lundy came in from wherever he had been with a can of Coors in his hand.

Renda said to him, "How many we got?"

Lundy wasn't sure at first what he was talking about, if he meant beers or what. But as he looked at Renda, he understood and said, "You and me for openers. I don't know when we're going, so I don't have anybody here. I thought after we talk about it, you know, see what you got in mind, I make a call and we get whatever we need."

"I think we need a truck," Renda said. "Good-size one. I'm not sure, but just in case we got to haul some people."

Lundy nodded. "Bobby Kopas's got one. Stake truck, open in back."

"All right," Renda said, then immediately shook his head. "No. Shit, I don't want him around. Get the truck tell him you're going to borrow it you'll bring it back, and get . . . four, five guys who know what they're doing."

"For when?"

"Tonight," Renda said. "Let's get it done before the fucking phone starts ringing again."

There was enough light in the packing shed to work by, but it was a dreary, bleak kind of light, like a light in a garage that didn't reach into the corners. A string of 100-watt bulbs, hanging beneath tin shades, extended the length of the conveyor that was bringing the melons in from the dock outside. The sound in the packing shed was the steady hum of the motor that drove the conveyor.

Most of the crew were outside, unloading the trailer. Nancy Chavez and Larry Mendoza's wife, Helen, did the sorting and were good at it, their hands deftly feeling, rolling the melons on the canvas belt, pulling out the ones that were badly bruised or overripe. Majestyk and Larry Mendoza were at the end of the line, packing the melons in cardboard cartons that bore the MAJESTYK BRAND label. Two other men in the crew were stacking the cartons, building a wall of them as high as they could reach.

By the time the trailer was unloaded it was almost ten o'clock. There were still melons on the conveyor, but Majestyk shut it down and said that was enough for one night, more than he'd expected they'd get done.

Mendoza came along the line to where his wife was standing and said, "I don't know, Vincent, but I think we're going to do it."

Nancy said, "If we can keep the grower working instead of goofing off, laying around in jail."

Majestyk was tired, but he felt good. He felt like talking to her and getting to know her. He said, "I remember—it seems to me somebody mentioned having a beer after work."

Nancy looked across the conveyor at him. "You still buying?"

"Sure, I'm going to be rich in about a week." He said to Mendoza, "Larry? How about you and Helen?"

"No, me and mama got more important things to do," Mendoza said, and slapped his wife on the can, making her jump a little and grin at them. "We're going to bed."

Nancy was still looking at Majestyk. "Maybe

you'd rather do that." As she saw him begin to smile, she added quickly, "I mean if you're tired."

Majestyk said, "Come on, let's go get a couple of cold ones." He was still smiling at her.

Harold Ritchie watched the headlights of the pickup approaching the highway and said to the deputy over by the tool shed, "Now where in the hell's he going?"

"If it's him," the deputy said.

"I guess I'm going to have to find out, aren't I?"

Ritchie walked over to the State Highway Department truck, grabbed the door handle and looked around again. " 'Less you want to this time. You been sittin' all day."

"You can talk plainer than that," the deputy said. "I'm about to go sit again. I think I got me some bad enchiladas or something."

He waited until Ritchie drove off before he went into the tool shed and radioed the Edna Post to let them know what was going on—which would be relayed to Lieutenant McAllen probably sitting home reading the paper or watching TV, a nice, clean, lighted bathroom down the hall from him, empty, nobody even using it.

Walking over to the portable toilet he was thinking, hell, he should've tailed the pickup this time, probably could've stopped at a gas station some-where, or a bar. Unbuckling his belt, the deputy stepped inside the toilet and closed the door.

Less than a hundred yards east of the construc-tion site three pair of headlights popped on.

The stake truck came first, followed by the two sedans, picking up speed, the truck reaching forty miles an hour by the time it got to the barricades, swerved in and sideswiped the portable toilet, the right front fender glancing off, scraping metal against metal, but the corner of the stake body catching it squarely, mashing into the light metal as it tore the structure from its base, carried it with forward momentum almost to the tool shed before it bounced end over end into the ditch. The stake truck kept going and turned into the road that led to Majestyk's place.

The two sedans, Lundy's Olds 98 and a dark-colored Dodge, came to a stop by the barricades, the Olds bathing the battered toilet in its headlight beams.

Renda and Lundy, and a third man with a ma-chine gun under his arm, got out of the cars and walked into the beam of light. When Lundy got the twisted door of the toilet open, straining to pull it free, the third man aimed his machine gun into the opening. Lundy pushed him aside, reached in with one arm and when he straightened again looked at Renda.

"Dead."

"Must've got hit by a truck," Renda said.

Pushing open the screen a little, Mendoza could see the stake truck in front of the migrant quarters and hear the low rumble of its engine. Just sitting there. Nobody had got out of the truck. Nobody had come out of the migrant quarters. They were all inside or around someplace close by because their cars were there, the three old junk heaps. When the two pair of headlights came down the road from the highway and passed the migrant quarters, Mendoza moved away from the doorway. He was wearing only his jockey shorts—maybe he should hurry up and put some clothes on. But the cars weren't coming to his place. They kept going.

Behind him his wife whispered, "Who are they? Do you know them?"

He knew. He was pretty sure he knew. But he said to her, "Stay with the children."

When she stepped into the doorway to look out he pulled her back because of the slip she wore as a nightgown. It showed dull white in the moonlight and he was afraid they would see her, even though he knew they were all the way to Vincent's house by now.

She said again, "Who are they?"

"I don't know," Mendoza answered. "But they

don't have any business with us and they're not friends I know of. Go to bed."

She lingered, but finally moved away from him. When he heard the springs and knew she was in bed again, he pushed open the screen door carefully and went outside, holding the door to close it, so it wouldn't make noise. On the steps of the porch, looking down the road, he could see the headlights of the two cars in front of Vincent's house. He didn't know if they were waiting or if they had gone inside. He said, God, why don't they leave? He's not there, they can see that, so go on, get out of here. Vincent was with a girl, talking, drinking beer. He could be gone for hours, having a good time; stay out late he could still get up early and work. They didn't know him.

He saw them in the headlights for a moment and faintly heard the car doors slam, then went into the house again as the cars came back this way. He was sure they were going to pass his house, leave, and when the cars turned in—coming straight at his house before stopping close to the porch—he couldn't believe it and began backing away from the screen door, but not soon enough. The headlights were blinding and he knew they could see him. He could hear the engines idling. Some men, three of them, dark shapes were coming up on the porch. When they came into the house he still couldn't see them because of the headlights.

One of them walked past him. He heard his wife's voice. "What do you want?" Frightened. He didn't hear the children.

Renda said, "Where is he?"

Mendoza thought of his wife and three children in the bedrooms, behind him. What was he? A guy standing in his underwear who just got waked up out of a sound sleep. How was he supposed to know what was going on?

He said, "I don't know. You mean Vincent Majestyk? Isn't he at home?"

He had never seen Eugene Lundy before and didn't see his features now, only a big shape that stepped up close to him. The next thing he knew he was hit in the mouth with a fist and felt the wall slam against his back. The man reached for him then and held him against the wall so he wouldn't fall down.

"Where is he?" Renda said again.

"I don't know," Mendoza said. "Believe me, I knew I'd tell you."

"He go into town?"

"I don't know," Mendoza said. "Honest to God, I thought he was home in bed."

Renda waited, knowing he was wasting time. The guy was probably telling the truth. He said, "Bring him along. And his wife."

They brought everybody out of the migrant quarters, pushing them to hurry up, making them stand in front of the place, in underwear or just pants, barefoot, squinting in the glare of the truck's headlights. Mendoza and his wife were pushed into the group by the men with guns in their hands who stood out of the light. The migrants waited, everyone too afraid to speak or ask what was going on.

Finally Lundy, who stood with Renda next to the truck, said to them, "We're looking for the boss. Who wants to tell me where he's at?" Lundy waited, giving them time. In the silence they could hear the crickets in the melon field. "Nobody knows, huh?" Lundy said then. "Nobody heard where he was going or saw him leave?"

Quietly, to Lundy, Renda said, "We got a dead cop and we're running out of time. Get rid of them."

Renda walked off into the darkness, toward the packing shed. He heard Lundy tell them, "You all've got two minutes to get in your cars and drive away from here and never come back." He heard one of the migrants say, a weak little voice with an accent, "We been working, but we haven't been paid yet. How we suppose to get paid?" And he heard Lundy say, "Keep talking, I'm going to start busting some heads. Now you people get the hell out of here. Now."

The doors of the packing shed were open. Renda went up the steps to the loading dock and looked inside. He could make out the conveyor and the melons on the canvas belt. He was curious about the place—as if the place might be able to tell him something about the man who owned it. Feeling along the wall inside the door, he found the light switch. Outside there was a sound of engines trying to start and finally turning over.

Lundy and the one with the machine gun came in. Renda was staring at the wall of cartons, the melons that had been sorted and packed that evening.

"Man's been busy," Lundy said.

"I said to him what do you want?" Renda continued to stare at the wall of melon cartons and Lundy and the one with the machine gun looked over at him. "He said I want to get my melons in," Renda went on. "That's all he wanted. Get his melons in."

Lundy couldn't believe it when he saw Frank pull out his .45 automatic—Christ almighty—and start firing it at the stacked-up melon cases, firing away, making an awful racket in the place, until his gun was empty.

Renda looked at them then. He seemed calm. His voice was, and said, "What're you waiting for?"

Lundy always did what he was told. It didn't have to make sense. He took out his big magnum and opened up at the cartons. Then the other one with the machine gun let go and the din was louder than before. They tore up the cartons, lacing them with bullet holes. Renda took the machine gun from the guy, turned to the conveyor, and shot up all the melons left on the canvas belt, blew them apart, scattering pieces all over the shed.

Christ, Lundy thought. He hoped Frank felt better now.

Kopas had been told they'd probably drop his truck off later that night, somewhere near the county road intersection west of Edna, where there was that Enco station on the corner and the café. Kopas asked what time. Lundy said, when they got back. But if they had to take some people somewhere—and Kopas had a hunch he meant the migrants—then he wouldn't get his truck back until morning.

But the migrants had cars. They could run them off in their own cars and not have to take them anywhere. So Kopas was pretty sure the truck would be back tonight.

He hung around the café-bar that evening, going outside and looking up the highway every once in a while. Being sure they had gone to Majestyk's place, he was anxious to know if they had killed him. If they hadn't been able to for some reason— and if Renda was with them—he was anxious for

Renda to see him again. Renda might decide he was a handy man to have around after all: he was alert, waited, did what he was told.

When Majestyk and the girl arrived, he was in the Men's Room of the café-bar. He came back into the room that was about half full of Chicanos and spotted Majestyk and the girl right away, sitting in a booth along the wall. He didn't see the two deputies at the bar—Ritchie and a deputy who had met him here—didn't notice them because they were in work clothes, and all Kopas was thinking about was getting out of there before Majestyk looked over. He glanced at the booth again as he went out the door—leaving the light and the smoke and the loud country steel-guitar beat inside—and saw Majestyk listening to something the girl was saying, giving her his full attention. Good.

He was more excited now than earlier in the day when he was out in the desert, the plane was taking off, and he was waiting to meet the famous Frank Renda. He saw Majestyk's pickup, parked a short way down from the café. He had a thought and began looking at the other cars, on both sides of the highway, and there it was, the State Highway Department truck. It was parked at the Enco station by the pumps; the station closed for the night.

Kopas started putting things together in his

mind. They hadn't gotten Majestyk because Majestyk was inside. Also a cop was in there, or around someplace. He was more anxious now than ever. He went across the highway and across the county road to wait there at the intersection, moving around, wanting them to hurry up and come before the guy left. About fifteen minutes passed. He was so anxious for them to come that, when he saw the three pair of headlights approaching, he knew it was them and couldn't be anyone else. The thing now was he had to act cool and hold down his excitement.

Lundy, slowing down for the intersection, saw the figure on the corner. He recognized the shirt, bright in the headlights, and the sunglasses and the curled-brim Texas hat. He said to Renda, next to him, "There's Bobby. He looks like he's got to take a leak or something."

Kopas was there as the car came to a stop, hunched down to look in the side window. He said, as calmly as he could, "Mr. Renda . . . man you want's inside that place over there, having a beer."

Renda said, "Alone?"

"With a girl. One works for him."

"Where's the cop sitting?" Renda said.

The good feeling was there and it was gone as he felt his confidence begin to drain out of him. Kopas straightened and, with a squinting, serious expression, looked over toward the State Highway Department truck parked at the gas station.

He said, "I'm not exactly sure yet, Mr. Renda. But you want me to, I'll find out."

He was not aware of the country music or the two deputies at the bar or the other people in the place. Not right now. His hand was on the bottle of beer, but he was not drinking it. He was looking at the girl's eyes, at the pearl earrings and the way her dark hair was parted on the side, without the bandana, and had a silver clip holding it back, away from her face.

Nancy said, "Do you mind my asking about her?"

"No, it's all right." Majestyk paused. "I don't know, I guess people change. Or else it turns out they're somebody else all the time and you didn't realize it. Do you think it's hard to know people?"

"Not always," Nancy said. "Was she blond, with blue eyes?"

"Most of the time blond. You put your hair up in rollers? You have very pretty hair."

"Once in a while I have. Why?"

"I picture my wife, I see her with rollers. She was always fooling with her hair, or washing it."

"You have any kids?"

"Little girl, seven."

"And you miss her."

"I guess I do. I haven't seen either of them in two years. They moved to Los Angeles."

A silence began to lengthen and Nancy said, "Are you thinking about them?"

"No, not really."

"What are you thinking about?"

"I'm thinking I'd like to know you better."

"Well, I'll fill out a personnel form," Nancy said. "Read it over, see if I pass."

"Always a little bit on the muscle." He was staring at her as he said, "You're very pretty."

"No, not very. But I suppose not bad-looking either. Not somebody you'd kick out of bed, huh, if that's what you've got in mind."

"Why don't you try and relax a little," Majestyk said, "and be yourself. Find out what it's like."

"You want to go to bed with me. Why don't you say it?"

"I'd like to hold you."

"See how close we can get?"

"Sometimes, hard as you try, you can't get close enough," he said. "You know that?" She didn't answer, but he knew by her expression, the soft smile, she was aware of the feeling. Wanting to lie very close to someone, holding each other, not saying anything, because they wouldn't have to use words to say it.

He said, "Let's go home, all right? Go to my house."

There was no need to make him wait. Or, as he said, to be on the muscle. She was aware that they knew each other, each other's feelings. She knew she could relax with him and be herself. Still she hesitated, she supposed out of habit, before saying to him, "All right, your house." She smiled then as he smiled. "But first I'll go to the Ladies'—if it isn't locked."

"If it is," he said, "I'll kick it open."

He watched her cross the room—and the men looking up at her as she passed their tables—to the little hall that led back to the kitchen and the rest rooms.

He saw a man come away from the jukebox and turn into the hallway and knew, even before the man with the hat and the sunglasses looked over his shoulder and grinned at him, it was Bobby Kopas. Majestyk started to slide out of the booth, rising. Then stopped, and sat down again as he felt the pressure of the hand on his shoulder.

"How you doing, buddy?"

Majestyk looked up, then past Renda toward the bar. "There're two cops sitting over there."

Renda took his time. He slid into the seat where Nancy had been and looked at Majestyk before saying, "If there weren't, you'd already be dead."

Majestyk's eyes went to the hallway again. Kopas was still there, watching.

"Leave the girl alone, all right? She doesn't have anything to do with this."

"I don't give a shit about the girl," Renda said. "As long as she stays in the can, out of the way. I got something to tell you. You probably already know it, but I want to make sure you do. I'm going to kill you."

"When?" Majestyk said.

"I don't know. It could be tomorrow. It could be next week." Renda spoke in a normal tone, quietly, without the sound of a threat in his voice. "You could hide in the basement of the police station, but I'm going to get you and you know it."

Majestyk raised the beer bottle and took a drink. Putting it down again his hand remained on the bottle and he seemed to study it thoughtfully before looking at Renda again.

"Can I ask you why?"

"I told you why. We make a deal or you're dead. The fact I got off has got nothing to do with it. You jammed me. You tried to, and nobody does that."

"I don't guess I can talk you out of it then, huh?"

"Jesus Christ—"

"Or there's anything I can do about it?"

"You can run," Renda said. "I'll find you. You can live at the police station. But you got to come out some time. There's no statute of limitations on this one. Whether I kill you tonight or a year from tonight, you're still going to be dead."

Majestyk nodded and was thoughtful again, fooling with the beer bottle. He said, "Well, I guess I got nothing to lose, have I?"

He raised the bottle in his left hand, but it was the right fist that did the job, hooked into Renda's face, in the moment he was distracted by the bottle, and slammed him back against the partition. There was no purpose in hitting him again or hitting him with the bottle. There was little satisfaction in it; but he was letting the guy know he wasn't a goat tied to a post. If Renda wanted him he was going to have to work for it.

The people at the next tables saw the blood and look of pure astonishment on Renda's face. They saw the expression begin to change as he touched his face, a dead expression that told nothing, but stared at Vincent Majestyk as he got up from the table.

They heard Majestyk lean over, his hands on the table, and say to the man he had hit, "Why don't you call the cops?" They watched him walk away as the man sat there.

Bobby Kopas didn't like it at all, what was happening now. Majestyk coming toward him. Renda, in the booth, who could stand up any second and

start blasting the guy. The two cops at the bar, trying to see past the people at the tables who were
standing now.

But nothing happened. Kopas stepped back as
Majestyk came into the hallway and went past
him—didn't even look at him—to the Ladies'
Room. He didn't do anything. Renda didn't. Nobody did. Majestyk pushed open the door to the
Ladies' Room and said to the girl who was standing there, "Let's go home."

It could have been a good night. Then there was no
chance of it being even a pretty good night. They
got back to the place to find no one there. Not even
Mendoza and his family. Majestyk saw the flares
and the flashing lights across the field, on the highway. The lights were there for some time before he
went over and found out a deputy had been killed.
Hit and run it looked like.

Harold Ritchie blew up when he saw Majestyk.
He said, "Goddamn it, you're the one started this!"

Majestyk said to him, "Listen, an hour ago I had
fourteen people at my place counting my foreman
and his family. Now everybody's gone, chased off
while you're sitting in a bar drinking beer."

"And a man was killed and we don't know who
done it because I had to watch *you*!" Ritchie yelled
at him.

There was no point standing on the highway arguing with a sheriff's deputy in the pink-red flickering light of the flares that had been set around the area.

Majestyk went home. He told Nancy what had happened, then told her to sleep in the bedroom, he'd sleep on the couch in the living room. When she objected he said, "I'm not going to argue with you. You're sleeping in there."

She didn't say any more and he didn't either. It wasn't until the next morning they found out what had been done inside the packing shed.

10

WHEN NANCY came into the shed, Majestyk was opening the cartons that were stitched with bullet holes and stained where juice from the melons had seeped out. She looked at the open cartons scattered about the floor, at the chunks of melon, yellow fragments, on the conveyor line.

"If he can't have you, he'll take your melons," the girl said. "How does it look?"

"Some are all right."

He walked past her, out to the loading dock, and stared at his empty fields and the pale morning sky. Some were all right. Spend a half day to sort them, maybe have one load to deliver to the broker. Most of the crop was still on the vines. If he could get it in he would at least break even and be able to try it again next year. If he could get the crop in. If he could get a crew. And if Renda would forget the whole thing and leave him alone.

But that was not going to happen, so he'd sit here and wait and watch the crop rot in the field.

Unless you could finish it somehow, Majestyk thought, and had a strange feeling as he thought it. Instead of waiting, what if there was something he could do to get it over with?

When he saw the figure walking in from the highway he knew it was Larry Mendoza—the slow, easy way he moved—and went down to the road to meet him. As Mendoza approached he held up his hand, as if to hold Majestyk off, knowing what was in his mind.

"Don't say nothing, Vincent. I live here, I work here. I took my wife and kids to her mother's, so they'd be out of the way. Now, what are we doing?"

"They hurt you," Majestyk said, staring at Mendoza's bruised, swollen mouth. "I'm sorry, Larry. I should have been here."

"No." Mendoza shook his head. "Getting that beer was the best thing you ever did."

"They asked you where I was and you wouldn't tell them," Majestyk said. "So they roughed you up."

"Not much. I only got hit once. Nobody else was hurt."

"You don't know if Frank Renda was one of them?"

"No, I never seen him, picture or nothing."

"Did you talk to the police?"

"Sure, a cop stop me in town, take me in. They ask some questions, but what do I tell them? Some men come, I don't even know who they are. I don't even *see* them. They tell us leave or get our heads busted. That's all. Come on, Vincent, we got some work, let's do it."

"If you'll do one thing for me, Larry," Majestyk said. "I think we got enough good melons for a load. Take the trailer into the warehouse and leave it there. You can come back later sometime, and get your personal things, your clothes and stuff."

Mendoza frowned. "What the hell are you talking about? I'll bring the trailer back, we'll pick melons and load it again. You retiring already, or what?"

"I can't ask you to stay here," Majestyk said.

"Then don't ask. I'll get the trailer."

As he started away Majestyk said to him, "Larry . . . it's good to see you."

When he returned to the packing shed Nancy had already begun the sorting, separating the undamaged melons and placing them in fresh cartons. She looked up as he came in.

"Lots of them are still good, Vincent. More than I thought."

"Larry's going to take a load in," Majestyk said. "He'll drop you off in town."

"What am I going to town for?"

He realized, by her expression, he was taking her by surprise. "To get a bus," Majestyk said. God, he sounded cold and impersonal, but went on with it.

"There's no reason now for you to stay. I'll pay you, give you money for the others in case you run into them." She came to her feet slowly, as he spoke.

"Last night you want to hold me," Nancy said, "see how close we can get. Today you want me to leave."

"Last night—that seems like a long time ago." He still didn't like his tone, but didn't know what to do about it. "I must've been nuts, or dreaming," he said, "believe the man'd sit and wait for me to get my crop in."

"All right, if you feel he's going to come back," the girl said, "then why don't we both leave?"

"Run and hide somewhere? He'd find me, sooner or later."

"So face it and get it over with, huh?" There was a sound of weariness in her tone. "Big brave man, has to stand alone and fight, no matter what. Where'd you learn to think like that?"

"You're not going to be here, so don't worry about it."

"Now you're mad."

"I don't have time to worry about it."

She said then, "I'll tell you something, Vincent. I've been in a car that was shot at and the man sitting next to me killed. Another time, a truck chased a bunch of us down a road, trying to run us over.

And once I was in a union hall when they threw in a fire bomb and shot the place up. I don't need anybody looking out for me. But if you want me to leave, if you don't want me here, that's something else."

He had to say it right away, without hesitating. "All right, I don't want you here."

"I don't believe you."

She was holding him with her eyes, trying to make him tell what he felt.

"I said Larry'll drop you off. Get your bag and be ready when he leaves." He stared at her, fought her eyes, until finally she walked past him, out of the shed.

They were lifting the battered portable toilet onto a flatbed truck with a hoist when Lieutenant McAllen arrived. He had them set the toilet back on the ground and looked at it, not touching it or saying anything until he turned to Harold Ritchie.

"How's it written up? Hit and run?"

"That's about all we can call it for the time being," Ritchie said.

McAllen nodded. "What're they going to do with it?"

"Scrap it, I guess. 'Less the road people want to bump it out."

"You think maybe it ought to be dusted first?"

"Well, we could. But there's people been handling it."

"I'm interested in the door," McAllen said. "Like maybe someone pulled it open, at the time I mean, to see if the man was alive or dead. There could be some prints along the inside edge."

"I guess there could be at that," Ritchie said.

"Let's bring it in and do it at home," McAllen said. "I think that'd be better than having a lot of people hanging around here, don't you?"

Ritchie was looking past McAllen, squinting a little in the glare. "Here comes his truck." As McAllen turned, Ritchie raised his binoculars. "Pulling a trailerload of melons. Going to market, like he didn't have a goddamn trouble in the world. No, it ain't him," Ritchie said then, as the truck reached the highway. "It's his hired man, Larry Mendoza, and looks like . . . some Mexican broad."

Mendoza paid attention to his driving, concentrating on it, and would keep busy looking at the trailerload of melons through the rearview mirror, because he didn't know what to say. The girl, Nancy, didn't say anything either—staring out the side window, her suitcase on the seat between them—but he was aware of her, could feel her there, and wished she would start talking about something.

He tried a couple of times to get it going, asking her if she thought she would run into her friends. She said probably, sooner or later. He asked her if she thought all the migrant farm workers would ever be organized and paid a living wage. She said again probably, someday.

It was too hard to make up something, to avoid thinking about Vincent and what was going on. So Mendoza didn't say any more until they crossed the state road intersection and he pulled to a stop opposite the café-bar.

He said then, "You don't mind waiting?"

"No, it's all right. I can get something to eat," she said, opening the door and putting a hand on her suitcase.

"Sure, get a beer, something to eat. The bus always stops there, so don't worry about missing it."

She said, "Thanks, Larry, and good luck."

"Good luck to you, too."

She closed the door and walked around the front of the truck. As she started across the highway, Mendoza said, "Nancy—"

She paused to look back at him.

"If he didn't have this trouble going on—"

"I know," she said.

"Come back and see us, all right?"

She nodded this time—maybe it was a nod, Mendoza wasn't sure. He watched her reach the sidewalk and go in the café-bar.

He drove on, into Edna, thinking about the girl and Vincent, the kind of girl Vincent ought to have. Especially Vincent. He didn't refer to Chicanos as Latins or look down at them in any way. It was easy to tell when someone looked down, even when he pretended to be sincere and friendly. Mendoza didn't busy himself with the trailerload of melons now, looking through the rearview mirror. He thought about Vincent and the trouble he was in, wondering what was going to happen. He didn't notice the Oldsmobile 98 following him.

Just past the water tower that said EDNA, HOME OF THE BRONCOS, Mendoza turned off the highway, crossed the railroad tracks, and drove along the line of produce warehouses and packing sheds. At a loading dock, where a man was sitting eating a sandwich, his lunch pail next to him, Mendoza came to a stop and said out the side window, "Where's your boss? Man, I got a load of top-grade melons."

The man on the loading dock wasn't in any hurry. He took a bite of his sandwich and chewed it before saying, "He's out to lunch. You'll have to wait till he gets back."

"What if I unload while I'm waiting?"

"You know he's got to check them first," the man on the dock said. "Go sit down somewhere, take it easy."

Well, if he had to. But he wasn't going to wait in the hot sun, or in the pickup that would get like an oven. And he wasn't going to sit with the guy on the dock and have to talk to him—he could tell the guy had it against Chicanos. So Mendoza got out of the truck and walked around the corner of the warehouse where there was a strip of shade about five feet wide along the wall.

He sat down with his back to it, tilted his straw hat down over his eyes and settled into a reasonably comfortable position. He pictured himself there as someone might come along and see him. Goddamn Mexican sleeping in the shade. Make him wait and then call him a lazy Mex something or other. He yawned. He was tired because he had gotten only about four hours sleep last night at Helen's mother's house, all of them crowded in there, two of the kids in bed with them. He wouldn't mind taking a nap for about a half hour, till the broker got back from his lunch.

His eyes were closed. Maybe he had been asleep, he wasn't sure. But when he opened his eyes he saw the front end of the Olds 98 rolling toward him— creeping, like it was sneaking up on him—from about thirty feet away.

Mendoza got up so fast his hat fell off. What the hell was going on? The whole wall empty and a car coming directly at where he was standing. Like some kind of joke. Somebody trying to scare him.

But he knew it wasn't a joke when he saw Bobby Kopas, the skinny, hunch-shouldered hotshot guy, coming along the wall toward him. He knew there would be another guy coming from the other side. Mendoza turned enough to look over his shoulder and there he was. It was too late to run. The car kept coming and didn't stop until it was only about three feet from him. Kopas and the guy on the other side came up to stand by the front fenders. He could smell the engine in the afternoon heat.

Kopas said, "Larry, I believe you were told to shag ass and don't come back. Ain't that right?"

"I was just helping out my friend a little bit, deliver some melons," Mendoza said.

"We give you a chance to run, you don't even take it."

"No, listen. I'm just doing this as a favor. I get rid of the load I'm gone, you never see me again."

"Larry," Kopas said, "don't bullshit me, okay?"

"Honest to God, I'm going to drop the melons and keep going."

"In the Polack's truck?"

"No, I told him I leave it here, so he can pick it up."

"Is that a fact? When's he coming?"

"I don't know. Sometime. Maybe tomorrow."

"How's he supposed to get here?"

"Hitchhike, I guess. He don't worry about that."

"Larry, you're shittin' me, aren't you?"

"Honest to God, ask the man in the warehouse,

around on the dock. Come on, let's ask him. He'll tell you."

"You aren't going nowhere," Kopas said. "You had your chance, Larry, you blew it."

The man behind the wheel of the Olds 98 hit the accelerator a couple of times, revving the engine. Mendoza looked at the car and at Kopas again quickly.

"Listen—what did I do to you? I worked for the guy that's all."

He saw Kopas step away and knew the car was coming as he stood with his back against the wall and no room, no direction, in which to run. He had to do something and jumped up, trying to raise his legs, but the car lunged into him, the bumper catching his legs and flattening him against the wall, holding him against it as he screamed and fell against the hood and then to the ground as the car went abruptly into reverse. He remembered thinking—the last thing as he tensed, squeezing his eyes closed—now the wheels were going to get him.

The hospital in Edna had an emergency room and eighteen beds, but it was more an outpatient clinic than a hospital and looked even more like a contemporary yellow-brick grade school.

For almost a year Majestyk had thought it was a

school. He had never been in the hospital before today—before the squad car picked him up and delivered him, blue lights flashing, to the emergency entrance where an ambulance and another squad car were waiting. Inside, the first person he saw was Harold Ritchie, the deputy coming toward him from the desk where a nurse's aide sat typing.

"Where's Larry?"

"Round the corner. I'll show you."

"What'd they do to him?"

"Guy at the warehouse—there was only one guy anywhere near where it happened—didn't see a thing. Not even the car."

"What'd they *do* to him?"

"Broke his legs," Ritchie said.

He was lying on a stretcher bed covered with a sheet, his wife with him, a curtain drawn, separating them from the next bed where a little boy was crying. A nurse, with a tray of test tubes and syringes, was drawing a blood sample from Mendoza's arm. Majestyk waited. Helen saw him then and came over and he put his arms around her.

"Helen . . . how is he?"

He could feel her head nod against his chest. Her voice, muffled, said, "The doctor say he's going to be all right. Vincent, you know what they did?"

He held her gently, patting her shoulder. "I know." He held her patiently because she needed his comfort, letting her relax and feel him close to her and know she was not alone. He heard Mendoza say, "Vincent?" and went over to the bed.

"Larry—God, I'm sorry."

"Vincent, I left the melons there."

"Don't worry about the melons."

"That's what I was going to say to you. Staying alive is more important than melons. Did you know that?" He seemed half asleep, his eyes closing and opening slowly.

Majestyk leaned in close to him. "Larry, who were they? You know them?"

"I think the same car as last night, the same people. And your friend, Bobby Kopas, he was there. Vincent, they not kidding. They do this to me, they going to kill you." Mendoza's face tightened as he held his breath, then let it out slowly before relaxing again. "Jesus, the pain when it comes—I never felt nothing like it."

"You want the nurse?"

"No, they already gave me something. They getting ready, going to set my legs."

"Larry, you're going to be all right. The doctor said so."

"I believe him."

"You go to sleep and wake up, it's done. You'll feel better."

Mendoza kept his eyes open, staring at Majestyk. He said, "You want me to feel better, Vincent? Tell me you'll go away. Hide somewhere.

There's nothing wrong doing that. Or, sure as hell, you going to be dead."

Harold Ritchie was in the waiting room, arms folded, leaning against the wall. He came alive when he saw Majestyk going past, heading for the door.

"Hey, what'd he say? He tell you anything?"

Majestyk kept going, pushing through the door.

Outside, he saw Lieutenant McAllen getting out of a squad car. He heard McAllen say, "Wait a minute!" And heard himself say, "Bullshit," not looking at the man or slowing down until McAllen said, "If you will, please. Just for a minute."

He waited for McAllen to come to him.

"Where you going?"

"Pick up my equipment."

"We'll drive you."

"I can walk."

McAllen paused. "I'm sorry about your hired man."

"He wasn't my hired man. He was my friend."

"All right, he was your friend." McAllen's tone changed as he said it, became dry, official. "I believe you know a deputy was killed last night, run over or beaten to death possibly, about the same time your migrants left. We'd like to locate them, talk to them."

"Why don't you talk to Frank Renda instead?"

"Because if we brought him in for questioning

he'd be out in an hour, and we wouldn't be any farther ahead."

"Where does he live? I'll talk to him."

"You would, wouldn't you?"

"Right now. Soon as I get a gun."

"We'll handle that," McAllen said. "The Phoenix police are watching both of his places, his house, his apartment. So far he hasn't been to either."

Majestyk stared at him. "You mean you don't know where he is? Christ, I was sitting with him last night. So were two of your deputies."

"They had to stay with you," McAllen said. "They radioed the post, but by the time a car got there Renda was gone. We know somebody's given him a place to stay. Probably in the mountains. But who, or where the place is, we don't know that yet."

"You don't know much of anything, do you?"

"I know I have a warrant with your name on it, and I can put you back in jail if you're tired of this."

"Or I can sit home and go broke," Majestyk said. "Why don't you just keep the hell out of the way for a while?"

"We pull out, you know what'll happen."

Majestyk nodded, as though he was thinking about it. "Well, let's see now. So far he's run off my crew, shot up a week's crop of melons and broke my friend's legs. So please don't give me any shit about police protection. Keep your hotshots and their flashing lights away from my property and maybe we can get this thing done and I can go back to work."

McAllen paused, studying Majestyk, as if trying to see into his mind, to understand him. He said, "Still worried about your melons. You're not going to get them picked if you're dead."

"And if I'm dead it won't matter, will it?"

"You want to bet your life against a melon crop—" McAllen paused again. "All right, you're on your own."

"I have been," Majestyk said, "from the beginning."

McAllen watched him walk off, down the drive toward the main street. He was thinking. The man seems simple, but he's not. He's easy to misjudge. He knows what he wants. He's willing to take risks. And he could already be planning something you haven't thought of yet. Mr. Majestyk, he was thinking, I'd like to know you better.

Ritchie had been waiting a few yards off to the side. He walked over now.

"We pulling out?"

"Let's let him think so," McAllen said, "and see what happens."

11

THE BROKER ACTED like he was doing him a favor, buying the trailerload of melons and waiting around after quitting time while Majestyk unloaded the cases himself because the warehousemen had gone home. He asked Majestyk how his hired man was. Majestyk told him Larry Mendoza was his friend, not his hired man. The broker said it must've been an accident. Mexican sleeping there in the shade, car comes along doesn't see him, rolls over his legs. Those people were always getting hurt with broken beer bottles and knives, the broker said. Now they were getting hurt while they slept. Majestyk didn't say anything. It was hard not to, but he held on and finally the broker went into his office. Later, when he picked up the check, he didn't say anything either. It was getting dark by the time he got out of there, heading home with the empty trailer.

Home. Nobody there now. A dark house at the end of a dirt road.

As he turned off the highway onto the road he looked at the rearview mirror, then out the side window to see the car that had been following him for several miles continue on. An Oldsmobile, it looked like.

He could hear crickets already in the settling darkness, nothing around to bother them. The packing shed was empty, Mendoza's house, the melon fields—driving past slowly, looking out at the dim fields the way he had looked at fields and rice paddies from the front seat of a jeep a dozen years before, feeling something then, expecting the unexpected and, for some reason, beginning to feel it again, now.

Majestyk drove up to within fifty yards of his house at the end of the road, stopped, turned the key off, put it in his pocket and waited a few moments, listening. When he got out he reached into the pickup bed for a wrench and used it to free the trailer hitch, crouched down between the pickup and the trailer where he could inch his gaze over the melon rows and study the dark mass of trees beyond his house. Pine trees. He didn't know what kind of trees he had watched twelve years ago, lying in the weeds not far from a Pathet Lao village after the H-34 helicopter had gone down, killing the pilot, the mechanic, and the ten Laotian soldiers. No, the trees were different. Only the feeling inside him, then and now, was the same.

* * *

Lundy cut his lights as he turned off the highway, hoping to hell he didn't get hung up on a stump or something. Once the road got into the trees it was all right. It was so narrow brush and tree limbs scraped the car on both sides, and the ruts were deep enough that he could feel his way along in the darkness and not worry about going off the road. He came up next to the Dodge parked in the small clearing, got out, and moved through the trees to where Bobby Kopas was watching the house.

Hearing him, Kopas looked over his shoulder. "He just come home."

"Who do you think I been following?" Lundy said. "Where is he?"

"By the truck. See him?"

It was about forty yards across a pasture to the house with its dark windows, and about the same distance again down the road to the pickup truck and trailer. Lundy held his gaze on the front end of the truck.

"I don't see him."

"Unhitching the trailer. He *was*."

"Well, where's he now?"

"Goddamn it, he was there a minute ago."

"He go in the house?"

"I'd have seen him."

Lundy looked around, getting an uneasy feeling. "Where're the others?"

Kopas pointed with his thumb. "Down there in the trees. So's to watch the side and back of the place."

"Later on," Lundy said, "we'll bring some more people in, seal him up." He looked at Kopas. "If he's still here."

"He's here. We can't see him is all. Down in behind the truck."

"I hope so," Lundy said. "You imagine what Frank would do to you if the man slipped out?"

He moved through the melon rows to the irrigation ditch and again, smelling the damp earth close to his face, experienced a feeling from the time before. It was easier this time because he wasn't carrying the M-15 and the sack of grenades. He wouldn't mind having the M-15 now, or the .30–.30 Marlin in the house or the 12-gauge Remington. The shotgun would be best, at night, at close range. He had thought of the gun when he thought of scouting the house and decided against it. He could be caught in the open too easily. It was better to look around first, make sure, and not approach the house until it was full dark. He reached the end of the irrigation ditch and came up behind the pump housing. From here, in the deep shadows, he was able to walk into the trees.

It had been midsummer when the pesticide tank truck came in through the back road to spray his outlying fields. Studying the trees he had remembered the road. It was a point to reach and follow, to help him keep his sense of direction. He remembered the clearing, too, and approached it through the dense trees and scrub as he had approached the village, smelling the wood smoke from a hundred meters away. He stopped when he heard the voice.

"I mean the man's got to be around, hasn't he? His truck's here. How's he going to go anyplace 'less he's in his truck?"

He knew the voice. There was another voice then, lower, and the sound of a car door slamming.

"Hey, I forgot to tell you—this afternoon, right after I got back—"

The familiar voice was drowned out by the car engine starting. Majestyk moved back into the trees. He waited. When the Olds 98 rolled past him he was close enough to touch it.

The deputy at the road repair site, sitting by the radio in the tool shed, said to the Edna Post, "His truck's still over there. Haven't seen nothing or heard a sound, so I judge he's home safely."

"Harold's about to leave," the voice coming over the radio said. "He wants to know what you want on your hamburgers."

"Mustard and relish," the deputy said.

"Mustard and relish, out."

"Out," the deputy said and flicked the switch off.

He heard the car coming and waited until it passed before stepping outside with the binoculars. So he saw only the tail-lights of the Olds, the lights becoming little red dots before they disappeared. He raised the binoculars putting them on Majestyk's house, inching them over to the trees and back again. It was too dark to see anything. Dark already, the melon grower was probably in bed, and here he hadn't even had his supper yet.

There were five of them watching the house. He came on them one at a time as he circled through the trees, passing them, seeing dark silhouettes, hearing a muffled cough. The last man was looking out of the trees toward the equipment shed and past it, across the yard, to the back of the house. Majestyk knew he could take the man from behind if he had to, with his hands. But he told himself no, as he had told himself the time before, circling the perimeter of the Pathet Lao village and almost running into the sentry—a young man or a boy who wore a cap with a short visor and held a Chicom machine gun across his skinny knees. He remembered the profile of the boy's face in the moonlight, the delicate features, and remembered wondering what the boy was thinking, if he was afraid, alone in the darkness. He could have shot him, cut his throat or broken his neck with his forearms. But he backtracked into the rain forest and waded for miles through a delta swamp so he wouldn't have to kill the boy. Maybe he had lost too much time and it was the reason they captured him the next morning as he slept, opening his eyes to see the muzzle of the Chicom in his face. He wasn't sure it was the reason he was caught; so he told himself it wasn't. They were on patrol and had stumbled across him.

There had been five of them then, as there were five now. They tied his arms behind him with hemp and looped it around his neck, to lead him back to the village or to another village. He was filthy and smelled from wading through the swamp. At a river he remembered was the Nam Lec, he asked if he could wash himself. One of them untied him and took him, with his Chicom, to the edge of the water. The rest sat on the bank ten yards away and began rolling cigarettes, leaning in toward the match one of them held, and the one guarding him was turned to watch them. Almost in one motion he grabbed the man by his collar, pulling him into the river, chopped him across the face with the side of his hand, took the Chicom away from him and shot two of the Pathet Lao with a single burst as they scrambled to raise their weapons. The three that were left he brought with him, thirty miles to the fire post at Hien Heup.

They gave him a Silver Star and a seventy-two-hour pass, which he spent in the bar at the Hotel Constellation in Vientiane. He told the story to a friend of his, another combat adviser sergeant, saying it didn't make sense, did it? Fall asleep and have to work your ass off to get out of a bad situation and they give you a medal. He remembered his friend saying, "You think people set out to win medals? They're just guys who fuck up and get lucky, that's all."

He was still glad, when he thought about it, he had not killed the sentry.

The one here, watching the back of the house, was nothing to worry about. Majestyk came out of the trees fifty yards down from the man, crossed at an angle so that the equipment shed would give him cover, and reached the side of the house without being seen. Then over the rail to the porch, where he waited a good minute, listening, before going in through the screen door.

In the dark he moved across the room to the cabinet where he kept his deer rifle and automatic shotgun, placed them on a long table behind the sofa that faced the front door, and went back to the cabinet for shells and cartridges. He began loading the shotgun first, thinking, You could go out the same way and take them one at a time. Except Bobby Kopas would be last and he'd run. Get them all together somehow. And Frank Renda, get him out there. That would be too much to ask, to have Renda waiting for him in the woods and not see him coming.

The sound was faint, the squeak of a floorboard, but clear in the silence. He came around with the shotgun at his hip, almost in the same moment he heard the sound, and put it squarely on the figure in the bedroom doorway.

"Don't shoot me, Vincent."

Nancy. He knew it before she spoke, seeing her size and shape against the light from the bedroom window, though not able to see her face. Her voice sounded calm.

"How'd you get here?"

"On the bus. It was going by—I went up to the driver and told him to stop. I told him I forgot something."

"You must've forgot your head. You know what you walked into?"

She didn't say anything. She had never heard this tone in his voice. Not loud, quiet, but God there was a cold edge to it, colder than it had been when he told her to leave.

"There are five men out there," Majestyk said. "With guns. They're not going to let me leave and they're not going to let you leave either. You got nothing to do with this, but now you're in it."

She said to him quietly, "So I guess you're stuck with me, Vincent."

After a moment, when he came over to her and put his hand on her shoulder, turning her in the doorway so that the light showed part of her face, she knew his tone would be different.

"Why did you come back?"

"I don't know," she said, and that was partly true. "Maybe see what it's like to be on the same side as the grower. That's a funny thing, Vincent. All my life I've been fighting against the growers. Now, this is different."

"You like to fight?" He kept watching her, making up his mind.

"You don't know me yet," Nancy said. "I like to do a lot of things."

He raised the barrel of the shotgun. "You know how to use this?"

"Show me and I will."

"How about a deer rifle?"

"Aim it and pull the trigger. Isn't that all you do?" She waited, looking up at him.

"I don't want you to be here," he said then, "but I'm glad you are. You understand what I mean?"

"You don't have to say anything. If I didn't know how you feel I wouldn't be here."

"You're that sure?"

She hesitated. "I hope so."

"You do have to leave yourself open, don't you? Take a chance."

"That's what it's all about."

"We'll have to talk about it again, when we have more time."

"Sure, it can wait." She smiled at him, even more sure of herself now.

"I'm going outside," he said. "Bring the truck up closer to the house—case they get it in mind to pull some wires."

"Are we going to make a run?"

"I don't know what we're going to do yet. First thing, I'll show you how to work the rifle." She followed him to the table and watched him as he began to load the Marlin. "If anybody tries to come in," he said, "shoot him. Don't say, 'Put up your hands' or anything like that, shoot him."

"All right, Vincent."

He handed her the rifle and picked up the shotgun again. "But make sure it isn't me."

* * *

Wiley was on the bearskin couch with her book. She looked up, over her reading glasses, at Lundy and said, "Gene's here."

Renda didn't pay any attention to her. He was on the phone again. Lundy had never seen a guy who was on the phone as much as Frank. The first time he ever met him—after doing seven on the armed robbery conviction and getting out and going to see him with the note his cellmate had given him— Frank was on the phone. It seemed like he had been on it ever since.

Right now he was listening, standing by the bar making a drink, the phone wedged in between his shoulder and his jaw. He put the scotch bottle down, picked up his drink, took some of it, then put the glass down hard and said, "What the fuck you talking about—I got back *yes*terday. Where's the wasted time? What if I was still in Mexico? You going to tell me everything would stop? Shit no." He listened again, moving about impatiently. "Look, it's a personal matter—you said so yourself. It's got nothing to do with the organization. I get it done and we get back to business. Not before."

He slammed the phone down and picked up his drink again. "Fucking lawyers. You don't know if they're working for you or you're working for them."

Wiley said, "I think your friends are worried you might get them involved."

"That's what I need, some more opinions."

She went back to her book as he turned to Lundy.

"What's he doing?"

"He picked up his trailer," Lundy said, "and went right home."

"Alone?"

"He *was*. But Bobby says there's a girl there. Come before he got back. I don't know," Lundy said, "man's waiting to get shot he's got some tail with him."

Put yourself in his place, Renda was thinking, and said, "The cops could've told him don't worry and he feels safe. Thinks, with all that's happened, I won't come for him right away."

"Whenever we do it," Lundy said, "we can't just walk in. The cops could be there waiting."

"You see any?"

"No, but they could've slipped in when it got dark. Be all over the place."

"I don't have time to fool around," Renda said. "They're starting to pressure me, give me some shit, tell me forget about the guy or hire it done."

Lundy agreed with them 100 percent, but he said, "You want to hit him yourself you got to wait for the right time, that's all."

"I don't *have* time! Can't you get that in your head?" He took a drink of scotch and calmed down a little. "How many guys you got there?"

"Five. In the trees by his place. There's a back road takes you in there." He watched Frank put his glass down and go over to a window that looked out on a dark patio and swimming pool.

When Renda turned to him again he said, "If it can take you in, nobody sees you, it can take him out, can't it?"

"If there's no cops in his house."

"All right, you watch his place. He tries to move during the night, stop him. We see who comes out in the morning. We don't see any cops around we grab him, put him in a car, take him out in the desert."

"What about the girl?" Lundy said.

"What girl?"

"The one with him."

"If she's with him she goes too."

Looking at the page in her book, Wiley wondered what the girl looked like. She wondered if the girl knew she might get killed. Or if the melon grower knew it. Yes, he'd know it, but she wasn't sure about the girl.

Lundy was gone. Frank was at the bar again making another drink. He was drinking too much, taking more pills than he ever had before.

Wiley said, "Do you ever worry about—that you could get caught by the police? Or shot? Or killed?"

"Are you going to give me some more opinions?"

"I was just curious. Is that all right?" He didn't

answer her and she said, "The guy really didn't mess you up that much, did he? I mean is it worth it? All the trouble?"

He turned from the bar with a fresh scotch.

"Is your book any good?"

"It's different."

"Good and dirty?"

"Dirty enough."

"Then why don't you read it?"

"And shut the fuck up."

"Right," Renda said, "and shut the fuck up."

For several minutes Majestyk stood by the screen door, holding it open a few inches, looking down the road toward the migrant quarters and the packing shed. He thought he had heard a car, not an engine sound but a squeak of springs rolling slowly over ruts. Now all he heard were the crickets. He looked out at his fields, past the pickup, that was parked about twenty feet from the porch now, facing the dirt road and the highway at the end of it. With his shotgun he moved to a side window and looked out at the dark mass of trees. There was no movement, no sound. He left the window.

From the bedroom doorway he could see the girl's profile against the window and the barrel of the Marlin.

"Anything?"

She shook her head. "I have trouble concentrating, Vincent. What I'd like to more than anything is straighten this place up."

"How can you see it in the dark?"

"When I came it was light. I never saw so much stuff not put away. Don't you hang anything up?"

"I haven't had much time for housekeeping. With one thing or another."

"What's that, on the other side of the bed?"

"Don't you know a deep-freeze when you see one? I got it secondhand for twenty-five bucks. Keep deer meat in it."

"I mean what's it doing in here?"

"What's the difference? You got to put it somewhere."

"You need help, Vincent. Well, maybe it's good you have it. They come, we can hide in it."

"They come shooting," he said, "we won't get a chance to hide. But if they *don't* come, soon, I lose a crop. I been thinking. He can wait a week, a year, long as he wants. But I can't wait anymore. So, I figure, I better get it done myself."

"Like turn it around?" She sounded interested.

"If I could spot him, bring him out—"

"Call him up," Nancy said. "Ask him to meet you someplace." There was enough light that she could see his expression, the smile beginning to form, and she said then, "I'm just kidding. I don't mean really do it. Come on, don't. You're just crazy enough to try."

"If he's watching us," Majestyk said, "I don't have to call him. And if he doesn't come tonight—" He paused. "I've got a half-assed idea that might be worth trying."

"God, you are going to turn it around, aren't you? Go after him instead of him after you."

"It's a thought, isn't it? Something he might not expect."

"God, Vincent, sometimes you scare me."

He smiled at her again, feeling pretty good considering everything, and went back into the living room.

12

BOBBY KOPAS SAID, "We got him for you, Mr. Renda. Sure'n hell he's in there and there ain't no way he can get out."

Renda stared at the house, at the early morning sun shining on the windows, waiting for some sign of life, wondering what the man was doing, if he was in there. The place looked deserted, worn out and left to rot. He was thinking that it would be getting hot in there. The guy should open a window, let in some air. The guy should be doing something, open the door, take the garbage out, something.

"He tries to go out the road," Lundy said, "we got two people down there in the packing shed. Another boy's over behind that trailer, see it? Case he tries to take off through the melon patch. Two more round the back. We cut his phone wire. I'd say all we got to do is walk up to the door and ring the bell."

"If he's there," Renda said. He looked at Kopas. "You seen him this morning?"

Bobby Kopas had been up all night, but he wasn't even tired. He'd been doing a job and hadn't made any mistakes. He said, "I figure he's locked himself in the toilet. Else he's hiding under the bed."

"I still have trouble, don't I," Renda said, "asking you a question?"

"What I meant, Mr. Renda, no, we haven't seen him yet, but he's in the house. His truck's right there. There's no place else he could be."

"And nobody's come by?"

"The girl," Lundy said, "yesterday. She's the only one."

Renda was staring at the house again. It wasn't Sunday. It wasn't a day off. The guy wasn't sleeping in. He should have come out by now. He should have been out an hour ago, working, doing something. So if he was in there he knew what was going on. He felt it or smelled it or had seen somebody.

"I don't like it," Renda said.

Eugene Lundy didn't like it either, not a bit; but it was a living that paid good money and gave him plenty of time to get drunk in between jobs. The thing to do was not think about it too much and just get the job over with. He said, "Well, we can stand here with our finger up our ass or we can go pull the son of a bitch out of there and get it done."

It was good to have people like Gene Lundy, they

were hard to find. "That's what we're going to do," Renda said, "but I don't want any fucking surprises. I don't need surprises. Gene, what have we got? What it looks like we've got. The guy in the house. He's got a girl with him. One, maybe two cops over on the highway. Are there more cops somewhere? You say no. All right, then what are the cops doing? Maybe they pulled out. Maybe they said fuck him. Maybe they don't give a shit about the guy and they don't care what happens to him. Except there's still a cop over on the highway. Gene, you're sure, right?"

Lundy nodded. "I saw him go in the tool shed. He's got a radio in there."

"All right," Renda said, "they know I'm going to hit him, they're hanging round. But they're not hanging around very close, are they? What're they doing?"

"Maybe," Lundy said, "they don't give a shit about the guy as you say. I don't know. Maybe they figure you were here, you're not going to come right back, they got a little time. I don't know how they think, fucking cops, but maybe that's what they think."

Renda took a minute, staring at the house. He nodded then and said, "Okay, we'll bring him out. We'll be quiet, go in and bring him out. Walk him back here to the car. And the girl. We'll have to take the girl."

Bobby Kopas had started to think about it too, the actual doing it, and he said, "Mr. Renda, what if he's got a gun?"

"He does, we take it away from him," Renda said. "He tries to use it, then we got no choice." He looked at Lundy. "Do it in the house and get out." He looked at Kopas then. "What I think we'll do— you walk up to the door first, we'll come in behind you."

Bobby Kopas heard it but didn't believe it. He said holy shit to himself and grinned because, Christ, he had never been in this kind of a set-up before and he didn't know how to act, what kind of a pose or anything. He felt like a dumb shit grinning, but what else was he going to do? He said, "Mr. Renda, I never done anything like this before. You know what I mean? I mean I might not be any good at it." Still grinning.

Renda said, "You walk up to the door, we come in behind you."

Majestyk put the two suitcases by the front door and looked at Nancy.

"You ready?"

"I guess so."

"Both bags go in the back of the truck. Save you time, and we might need the one sooner than I'd like."

"All right."

"Once you start, put your foot on it. Don't stop or slow down. Somebody gets in your way, run him over. Five or six miles down the highway you'll see the Enco sign on the corner. The café's right past it."

"Vincent—"

"Listen to me. You get out, take your suitcase, and walk over to the café."

"Vincent, please, you can't do it alone. You need someone."

"Think about what you have to do," he said. "That's enough. More than I have a right to ask."

"Please take me with you."

"I'm not going to argue with you," Majestyk said. "We've discussed it. I'm not going to change my mind now. You get off and I keep going and that's the way it's going to be."

"All right," Nancy said, "but you feel something, Vincent, the same as I do. You can't tell me you don't."

He opened the door and stepped back from it, out of the way. He said, "It's time to go."

They watched her come out with the suitcases and swing them, one at a time, into the back of the pickup. When she got in behind the wheel Lundy said, surprised, "She's taking off in his truck."

"Two suitcases," Renda said. He had to make up his mind right now. Stop her or let her go. The guy could be making her leave, getting her out of the way. Or the guy could be pulling something. He said to Kopas, "She have a suitcase yesterday?"

"Hey, that's right," Kopas said. "She did."

"How many?"

"Just one. Yeah, walked all the way across the field with it."

They heard her voice as she called something to the house. Her arm came out of the window and waved. As the truck started to roll away from the house Lundy said, "She's leaving him there. You believe it?"

Right now, Renda was thinking. Stop her. Yell to the guy behind the trailer. Yell at him to stop her, pull her out of the truck. But even as he made up his mind and screamed it, "Get her! Stop the truck!" it was too late.

Majestyk was out of the house, running, chasing the pickup, catching the tailgate with his hands and rolling over it into the box as the truck roared off, raising a trail of dust.

Nancy caught only a glimpse of the one by the melon trailer. He was stepping into the road, raising a gun, then jumping aside, away from the front fender, and she was past him, her hands tight on the vibrating wheel, wondering if Vincent was being bounced to death on the metal floor of the box. She wanted to look around, but she kept her eyes on the road, doing fifty now and suddenly seeing the car coming out from the side of the packing shed, coming fast and braking, skidding a little as it reached the narrow road and sat there blocking the way. Nancy cranked the wheel hard to the right, swerved around the front of the car, in and out of the ditch and back onto the road. In the rearview mirror she saw the car back up and make a tight turn to come after her. She was approaching the highway now and would have to slow down.

Turn left and race the five or six miles to Edna. Get out at the café and take her suitcase while he jumped in behind the wheel and before she could say anything he would be gone, leading them up into the mountains somewhere and she would never see him again.

He couldn't do it alone. He needed her. The two of them might have a chance, but he was stubborn and wouldn't listen to her. So she could be meek and do what she was told and never see him after he got in the truck and she walked across the street to wait for the bus. Or—she could forget his instructions, everything he had said, and help him, whether he wanted her to or not. It was simple, already decided. When she reached the highway she turned right instead of left.

He was pounding on the window, yelling at her, "It's the other way! Where in the hell are you going?"

She looked over her shoulder and gave him a nice smile, mashed the accelerator, and saw him fall off balance, away from the window.

The deputy at the road construction site saw him raise up again, just as the pickup was going by, and press against the truck's cab, by the back window. The deputy knew it was Majestyk. But he didn't get a good look at who was driving. He thought it was the girl, but he couldn't be sure. The truck went by so fast—west, away from Edna. He was on the radio when the car came out of the road—dark green Dodge, two-door model—squealed out, turning hard, and there wasn't any question in his mind somebody was after somebody.

Thirty seconds later Harold Ritchie was in McAllen's office.

"Renda or some of his people are hot after him. Going east on the highway."

"Now you're talking," McAllen said. "Let's put everything we got on it."

He knew what she was doing now, and knew what he had to do. Lying on his side in the pickup bed he opened his suitcase, took out the stock and barrel of the Remington 12-gauge, got them fitted together and shoved in five loads. It wasn't easy; it took him longer than usual, because of the metal vibrating beneath him and the sway of the truck and the wind. It was hard to keep his balance, propped on an elbow, hard to keep the shotgun steady and the shells in one place.

The crazy girl was having it her way. He saw her face a couple of times, looking over her shoulder through the window, seeing if he was ready.

He needed more time to get the Marlin put together and loaded.

But the dark green car was coming up on them fast. The truck could do maybe eighty, the car a hundred and twenty probably, or more. It wouldn't be long before it was running up their rear end. He looked back again, as they reached the lower end of a grade, and now saw two more cars behind the green one, closing in from about a half to a quarter of a mile away.

Nancy's eyes moved from the outside rearview mirror to the road ahead, the narrow blacktop racing at her, a straight line pointing through scrub and pasture land. On the left side of the road was a stock fence, miles of wire and posts and up ahead, finally, there it was, a side road. Higher posts marked the road. And a closed gate hung across the entrance.

There wouldn't be time to stop and open the gate. She knew that.

There wouldn't be time to load the Marlin. Majestyk realized that now. He put it down quickly, across the open suitcase, and picked up the shotgun again. He had to get turned around, face the tailgate.

He was moving, keeping low, on his elbows and knees—and was thrown hard against the side of the pickup box as the truck left the road and its high four-wheel-drive front end smashed through the wooden gate, exploded through it with the sound of boards splitting, ripped apart by the high metal bumper.

By the time Renda's three cars were through the gate and had come to a sudden stop, the truck was bounding across the desert pasture, making its own trail, running free where the cars couldn't follow.

No one had to say it. The rocks and holes, steep-banked washes and scrub, would rip the under-body of an automobile, tear out the suspension. They sat staring at the dust settling and the yellow speck out there in the open sunlight—Renda in the front seat with Lundy, Kopas in back.

"There's a road over there," Renda said finally. "They got to be headed for something."

"Taking a shortcut," Lundy said.

"There is one," Kopas said, "if I remember correctly. About a mile, county road cuts through there, goes up in the mountains."

The three cars turned in a tight circle and went out through the gate the way they had come in, the dark green Dodge leading off.

Within five miles the county blacktop began to wind and climb, making its way up into high country.

Majestyk felt better now. He had a little time to breathe and knew what he was going to do. The girl had set it up for him, given him the time. She had said he needed her and she was right. When he signaled to her and she stopped, he got out of the box and came up on her side.

"I guess there's no way to get rid of you, is there?"

"I told you before, Vincent, you're stuck with me."

She was the one to have along all right, but he couldn't think about her now. He told her to hold it about thirty-five, let them catch up again. He got back into the rear end and that was the last thing he said to her for a while.

There were a few new melon cartons in the pickup bed, flat pieces of cardboard he put under him for some cushion, soften the damn skid strips on the floor. Then he put the two suitcases at the back end of the pickup box, against the tailgate, and rested the shotgun on them. Lying belly down they were just about the right height. He reached up and pulled the latch open on one side of the tailgate. The other one would hold the gate closed until he was ready.

When he saw the three cars coming again, they were on a good stretch of road, straight and climbing, a pinyon slope rising above them on the right and a steep bank of shale and scrub that fell off to the left, dropping fifty or more feet into dense growth, dusty stands of mesquite.

Now he would have to keep down and rely on Nancy. In the window he saw her look back at him and nod. That meant they were coming up fast. He could hear the car.

Nancy was watching it in the rearview mirror—catching glimpses of the other two cars behind it—letting them come, watching the first car closely to see what it was going to do and trying to hold the truck steady on the narrow road. The car was fifty, forty feet away, crawling up on the truck, overtaking it and beginning to pull out, as if to pass. She held up two fingers in the rear window, a peace sign.

Majestyk was ready. He reached for the tailgate latch, pulled the chain off. The gate dropped, clanged open and there was the dark green Dodge

charging at him, a little off to the right. At twenty
feet Majestyk put his face to the shotgun, fired
three times and saw the windshield explode and the
car go out of control. It swerved across the road,
sweeping past the tailgate, hit the bank on the right
side and came back again—as the two cars behind,
suddenly close, braked and fishtailed to keep from
piling into the Dodge. The car veered sharply to the
left, jumped the shoulder, and dived into the brush
fifty feet below.

He fired twice at the second car, the Olds 98, but
it was swerving to avoid hitting the bank. The shot
raked its side and caught part of the third car, taking out a headlight, as the car rammed into the left
rear fender of the Olds, kicked it sideways and both
cars came to a hard abrupt stop.

Majestyk gave Nancy the sign, felt the pickup
lurch as it shifted and took off, leaving the two cars
piled up in the road.

The first thing Lundy did, he went over to the
shoulder to look down at the Dodge, at the rear end
of it sticking out of the brush. There was no sign of
the two guys. They were probably still inside. He
couldn't see how they could be alive, but it was
possible. Lundy was starting down the bank when
Renda called him.

"Gene, come on." Renda was walking away from

the rear of the Olds. The other car was slowly backing up. He said, "We're okay. Let's go."

Lundy began to say, "I was thinking we ought
to—don't you think we should take a look?"

"We're going to get in the car, Gene, and not
waste any more time. Now come on."

"They could be alive. Hurt pretty bad, caught in
there."

"I don't give a shit what they are. We got something to do, right now, before he gets someplace
and hides."

Renda didn't say any more until they were in the
car, following the road up through the pinyon, looking at side trails, openings in the trees where he could
have turned off. But there wasn't any way to tell.

"That goddamn truck of his, he can go anywhere," Renda said. "He knows this country. He
told me, he comes up here hunting."

"If he knows it and we don't," Lundy said, "it
changes things."

"I don't know, is he running or what? The son of
a bitch."

"If he's still on this road," Lundy said, "we'll
catch him. Otherwise I don't know either."

There was a game trail nearby where he had sat
with the Marlin across his lap and waited for deer:

meat for the winter, to be stored in his twenty-five-dollar deep-freeze. He wondered if he would go hunting this fall. If the girl would still be here. If either of them would be here.

He sat with the Marlin now as he had sat before, this time looking down the slope, through the pine trees to the road, the narrow black winding line far below. The cabin was less than a mile from here. He wondered if Renda would think of it and remember how to find it. No, he wouldn't have picked out landmarks and memorized them. He was from a world that didn't use landmarks.

He said to the girl, "Did you ever shoot a deer?"

"I don't think I could."

"What if you were hungry?"

"I still couldn't."

"You eat beef."

"But I don't have to kill it."

"All right, I'll make you a deal. I'll shoot it, you cook it."

"When are we going to do that, Vincent?"

"In a couple of months. We'll have plenty of time. Sit around, drink beer, watch TV. Maybe take some trips."

"Where do you want to go?"

"I don't care. Anyplace."

"We going to get married first?"

"Yeah, you want to?"

"I guess we might as well, Vincent. Soon as we get some time."

Looking down the slope he said, "Here come a couple of friends of ours."

They watched the two cars pass below them on the winding road.

"Now what, Vincent?"

"Now we give them a kick in the ass," Majestyk said.

Renda's three men in the second car, following the Olds, were in general agreement that riding around in the mountains was a bunch of shit. That Frank Renda ought to take care of his own hit, if he wanted the guy so bad. That maybe they should stop on the way back—if they ever got out of this fucking place—and see about the two guys who went over the side. Though they must be dead; nobody had yelled for help. They were looking out the windows, up and down the slopes, but if the guy wasn't still on the road they knew they weren't going to find him. How could they get to him?

The one in the back seat said, "There shouldn't be nothing to it. Wait for the right time you can set the fucking guy on fire, do it any way you want. This hurry-up shit doesn't make any sense."

"You know what the trouble is?" the driver said. "The guy, the farmer, he doesn't know what he's doing. He shouldn't even still be around."

"That's it," the one in the back seat said. "If he knew anything he'd know enough not to be here. It's like some clown never been in the ring before. He's so clumsy, does so many wrong things, you can't hit the son of a bitch."

"Fighting a southpaw," the driver said. "You ever fight a southpaw?"

"You get used to that," the one in the back seat said. "I'm talking about a clown. Hayseed, doesn't even own a cup."

"So you know where to hit him," the driver said.

"Shit, try and get to the guy."

Talking about nothing, passing the time. The one in the back seat looked out the side window at the dun-colored slopes and rock formations. They were getting pretty high, moving along a hogback, the spine of a slope. He half turned to look out the back window and said, "Jesus!" loud enough to bring the driver's eyes to the rearview mirror and the man next to him around on the seat.

The high front end of Majestyk's pickup was on top of them, headlights and yellow sheetmetal framed in the back window, the guy behind the

wheel looking right at them, saying something, and
the girl next to him ducking down.

Majestyk pressed down on the gas, caught up and
drove the high bumper into the car's rear deck. He
saw the car beginning to pull away, pressed the gas
pedal all the way to the floor and caught the rear
end again, stayed with it this time, fighting the
wheel to keep the car solidly in front of him, ram-
ming it, bulldozing it down the narrow grade, hitting a shoulder and raising dust, hanging with it,
seeing sky above the car and knowing what was
coming, foot pressed hard on the gas for another
five seconds before he raised it and mashed it down
on the brake pedal.

The car almost made the turn. It skidded sideways, power-sliding, hit the shoulder, and went
through the guardrail turned onced in the air and
exploded in flames five hundred feet below.

Majestyk was through the turn, saw the Olds 98
on the road three switchbacks below him, came to
an abrupt stop, turned around, and headed back
the way they had come, aware of the smoke now
billowing up out of the canyon. He was sure Renda
heard the explosion and would be coming back. So
he'd go up into the pines again and work out the
next step.

In the quiet of the cab he heard Nancy say, "I hope you never get mad at me, Vincent."

The Olds 98 came to a stop in the shadow of a high, seamed outcropping of rock. The shadow covered the road that continued in dimness, reaching a wall of rock and brush before bearing in a sharp curve to the right.

Lundy got the map out of the glove box and spread it open over the steering wheel. It was quiet in the car, except for the sound of Lundy straightening the map, smoothing the folds.

Renda stared straight ahead, through the windshield. We haven't been out here an hour, he was thinking, and he's killing us. Do you know what he's doing? Do you see it now?

Bobby Kopas fidgeted in the back seat, looking out the window on one side and then the other, bending down to see the crest of the high rocks. It was so quiet. Sunlight up there and shade down here. Nothing moving.

"His hunting country," Renda said. "He brought us here."

"I see where we're at," Lundy said. "The lodge is only about six, eight miles west of here, but roundabout to get to. 'Less we want to go all the way back to the highway, which I don't think is a good idea."

Renda wasn't listening to him. He was picturing a man in work clothes and scuffed lace-up boots, a farmer, a man who lived by himself and grew melons and didn't say much.

"He set us up," Renda said. "The farmboy knew what he was doing all the time and he set . . . us . . . up."

Lundy said, "What do you want to do? Go back to the lodge? I don't see any sense in messing around here." He waited, watching Renda stare out the window. "Frank, what do you want to do?"

He didn't know. He realized now he didn't know anything about the man. It was like meeting him, out here, for the first time. He should have known there was someone else, another person, inside the farmer. The stunt the guy pulled with the bus and trying to take him in, make a deal. That wasn't a farmer. He had been too anxious to get the guy and had not taken time to think about him, study him and find out who he was inside.

Lundy said, "There's no sense sitting here."

Renda continued to stare at the wall of rock ahead of them, where the road curved, thinking of the man, trying to remember the things he had said, trying to out-think him now, before it was too late. He didn't see the figure standing on the crest of the rocks, not at first. And when he saw him he was a shadow that moved, a dark figure silhouetted against the sky a hundred yards away, holding something, raising it.

"Get out of here!"

Renda screamed it, Lundy looked up and the rifle shot drilled through the windshield and into the seat between them with a high whining sound that was outside, far away. The second shot tore through the glass two inches from the first and Renda screamed it again, "Get out of here!"

Majestyk put four more .30–30's into the car before it got around the bend and was out of sight. He might have hit one of them but he doubted it. He should have taken a little more time on the second shot, corrected and placed it over to the left more. That's what you get, you don't hunt in a year you forget how your weapons act.

He walked away from the crest, back into the pines where Nancy was waiting by the truck, shaking his head as he approached her.

"Missed. Now I got to bird-dog him."

"Now?" She seemed a little surprised. "How can you catch up with him?"

"I can cross-country, he can't."

"You're really going after him?"

"We're this far," he said and watched her cock her head, then look up through the pine branches.

"I think I hear a plane," she said. "You hear it?"

He heard it. Walking back from the crest into the trees he had heard it. "You'll see it in about a minute," he said. "Only it's not a plane, it's a helicopter."

Harold Ritchie had radioed ahead to cars patrolling the main roads as far as thirty miles east of Edna. They reported, during the next half hour, no sign of a yellow four-wheel-drive pickup, with or without anybody chasing it.

So he must have taken them up in the mountains, Lieutenant McAllen decided, and called the Phoenix Police for a helicopter. Get more ground covered in an hour than they could in a week.

It didn't even take that long. McAllen and Ritchie had been cruising the highway and some of the back roads. They were at the road repair site when the chopper radioed in. There was static and the sound of the rotor beating the air, but the pilot's voice was clear enough.

"Three-four Bravo, this is three-four Bravo. I believe we got him. Yellow pickup truck heading south, in the general direction of county road 201, just west of Santos Rim, God almighty, or else it's a mountain goat. I thought he was on a trail, but there ain't anything there. He's bouncing over the rocks, flying. Heading down through a wash now like it's a chute-the-chute. Look at that son of a bitch go!"

McAllen and Ritchie looked at one another. They didn't say anything.

"On 201 now heading west," the pilot's voice said. There was a pause. "Hey, we got something else. Looks like . . . an Oldsmobile or a Buick, late model, dark blue . . . about a half mile out in front of the pickup, going like hell. Let me get down closer. This is three-four Bravo out."

Lieutenant McAllen looked up in the sunlight, toward the mountains, then at Harold Ritchie. "You don't suppose—"

"I'd more likely suppose it than not," Ritchie said.

They heard the radio crackle and the helicopter pilot's voice came on again.

"This is three-four Bravo. Looks like they pulled a disappearing act on us. I don't see either one of them now. They must've turned off on a trail through the timber. Hang on I'll give you some coordinates."

"About how far away are we talking about?" McAllen asked Ritchie. "The general area."

"Not far. Take us twenty, thirty minutes, depending on the coordinates he gives us."

"Then we'd still have to find them," McAllen said.

"We get enough cars up there," Ritchie said, "we can do it."

"But can we do it in time?"

Ritchie wasn't sure what he meant. "In time for what?"

"In time to keep him from killing himself," McAllen said.

13

WILEY WAS BORED. She had finished her book. There wasn't anything else to read in the place but business and banking magazines and a few old *Playboys*. It was a little too cold to go in the pool—which wasn't much of a thrill even when it was warm. She was tired of lying in the sun but not tired enough to take a nap. The whole thing, lying around swimming pools, waiting, was getting to be a big goddamn bore.

And the ice in her iced tea had melted. She put the glass on the cement next to the lounge chair, snapped her orange bikini bottom a little higher on her can as she got up and went into the lodge, or whatever it was, that Frank said looked like a dude ranch.

It did look like a dude ranch. All those Indian blankets and animals looking out of the wall. She turned the hi-fi on, got some rock music she liked but didn't recognize and was patting her bare thighs gently, keeping time, when Frank came in the front door. Frank and Gene and the new one, the little smartass carrying a shotgun. She hadn't heard the car drive up.

"Well, hey. What's going on?"

The three of them were at the front windows, not paying any attention to her.

"I never seem to catch the beginning," Wiley said. "Will somebody tell me what's going on?"

She moved over a little, her hips keeping time with the music, to be able to look out the window, past Frank and across the open yard to where the long driveway came in through the trees. She didn't see the Olds; then she did—over to the side a little at the edge of the trees, as if hidden there. They were waiting for someone to come up the drive and as she realized this her hips stopped keeping time and she thought of the police.

"You think," Wiley said, "I should start packing or what?"

"He's in the trees," Renda said.

"He could be," Lundy said, "if he saw us turn. But maybe he didn't."

Renda looked over his shoulder at Wiley. "Give me the glasses. Over on the table."

"Would you mind telling me something?"

"Give me the *glasses*."

He raised the window and got down on his knees, took the binoculars as she handed them to him and rested his elbows on the sill. The trees were close to him now, dark in there but clearly defined as he adjusted the focus, scanned slowly toward the drive, held for a while, trying to see down the length of the dirt road, then back again, slowly. He stopped. From the side of a tree about twenty feet into the woods, Majestyk was aiming a rifle at him.

With the sound of the shot, the glass above his head shattered. Renda dropped below the sill to his hands and knees, in a crouch. There was a silence before he heard the man's voice, coming from the trees.

"Frank, let's finish it. Come on, I got work to do."

Wiley watched Frank crawl from beneath the window and stand up, turning to put his back against the wall. She expected him to yell something at the guy, answer him, but he didn't. He was looking at her with a thoughtful sort of pleased expression; not really happy, but relaxed as he drew a .45 automatic from underneath his jacket. She still didn't know what was going on.

Majestyk handed Nancy the rifle and picked up the shotgun, leaning against a tree, as he saw the front door open.

Wiley came out in her orange bikini. She seemed

at ease, even though she was looking around, more curious than afraid. Coming across the lawn she said, "Where are you?"

"Over here," Majestyk said. He saw her gaze turn this way, but was sure she couldn't see him yet.

"Frank's not home," Wiley said. "You want to come in and wait?" He didn't answer now and she turned to go. "Well, it was nice talking to you."

"Wiley—"

She stopped and looked back. "Yeah?"

"Come here."

"I don't know where you are."

"Over here. That's right."

He waited until she was in the trees, more cautious now, and finally saw where they were standing. "What's he doing?" Majestyk said. "He want you to point to me so he can shoot?"

"I told you, he's not home."

"The car's over there."

"It belongs to somebody else."

"Wiley, tell Frank the cops are on the way. Tell him if he wants to settle it he hasn't got much time."

She hesitated. "Police, huh. Listen, this really hasn't got anything to do with me. I just happen to stop by."

"Who else is in there? How many?"

She hesitated again. "Just Frank . . . and two others. God, he's going to kill me."

Majestyk turned to Nancy. "Put her in the truck. Drive back to the road and wait for me there."

Wiley said to Nancy, "I really don't know what's going on. I don't have any clothes or anything."

"Don't worry, I'll give you a nice outfit," Nancy said, and looked at Majestyk again. "Vincent, wait for the police, all right?"

"If they come," he said, "but right now it's still up to him."

They couldn't see her now. There had been a spot of orange in the trees, but now that was gone. "Where'd she go?" Kopas said. He didn't like it at all. Five people dead, the man out there waiting for them. The man must be crazy, all he'd done.

"He grabbed her," Lundy said. He was holding his big magnum, resting it on the windowsill.

Why would he? Kopas was thinking and said, "Maybe they left. He sees we got him, so he took her and cut out."

"He's there," Renda said, sure of it now, since he had begun to know the man, understand him. "Son of a bitch, we got to suck him out. Or go in after him."

Kopas said, "You mean walk out there?"

Renda looked at him. "If I tell you to."

* * *

Majestyk came up to the Olds 98 through the trees, keeping low, and there was nothing to it. The next part he'd have to do and not worry about and if they spotted him and fired he'd have to back off and think of something else. He opened the front door on the passenger side, waited a moment, then slid in headfirst over the seat and pulled the key out of the ignition. Coming out he looked at the back-rest of the seat cushion, at the two bullet holes that were hardly noticeable. Just a little more to the left. He wished he'd taken a couple more seconds. It would have saved him a lot of trouble.

They could still come out the front while he worked around through the trees to the back, but it wouldn't do them any good now. They weren't go-ing anywhere, unless on foot, and then it would be even easier.

That's what he did: cut across the open to the blind side of the house and stayed close to it as he made his way around to the patio.

It could work because they wouldn't expect him. Get up to a window or the glass door underneath the sundeck, shove the pump gun in, and wait for somebody to turn around. He moved past the lounge chair Wiley had been using a little while be-fore, his eyes on the window. Even if he had looked down then he might not have seen the iced tea glass, it was so close to the chair. By the time he did see it he had kicked it over—hearing it like a window breaking—and all he saw were the broken fragments and a piece of lemon on the wet cement.

Renda turned from the front window. He stood listening, holding the .45 automatic at his side, then raised it as he started across the room toward the patio door. Lundy followed him.

Kopas waited. He wasn't sure he wanted to go over there. He watched Renda press against the glass panes to look out, trying to see down the outside wall of the house. Kopas knew he'd have to open the door and stick his head out to see anything. He wondered if Renda would open the door, if he'd go out. Christ, it would take guts.

He heard Renda say to Lundy, "You stay here. I'm going up on the sundeck. I spot him I'll yell to you."

Lundy nodded, holding the big mag, and moved in close to the door as Renda came back across the room. Kopas still didn't know what to do. He was sure, though, he didn't like being here with the guy right outside, the guy maybe poking a gun in a window any minute.

That is why he followed Renda to the front hall and up the stairs. The guy couldn't poke a gun into a second-floor window.

Renda went into a bedroom and over to the sliding glass door that opened on the sundeck. He glanced at Kopas as he went out, noticing him, but didn't say anything—like other times, looking through him as if he wasn't there.

Kopas said, "What you want me to do, Mr. Renda?"

Maybe Renda hadn't heard him. He was out on the sundeck now, looking over the railing at the patio. Kopas raised his shotgun and moved to the open doorway. He didn't go out. He could see most of the patio and the swimming pool, the sun reflecting on the clear green water. He watched Renda go to his hands and knees, trying to see down through the narrow spaces between the deck boards. Renda crawled along this way, coming back to the door before he got to his feet again.

"Son of a bitch, he's under there," Renda said.

But where? Kopas was thinking. The deck was about thirty feet long. He could be right underneath them or he could be down a ways or hiding behind something. He watched Renda move to the rail again, then look over to the left, to where the patio door would be, where Lundy was waiting. He watched Renda lean over the rail and point the .45 straight down—and couldn't believe it when Renda suddenly yelled out.

"Gene, he's going around the side! Get him!"

*　*　*

Majestyk's eyes were raised to the sundeck above his head, his shotgun pointing straight up to where he was pretty sure Renda was standing—where he had heard the movement and where the glints of sunlight between the boards were blotted out.

He didn't know it was Renda, not until he heard Renda's voice, his words clear, startling. And heard something else. A door. Quick footsteps on cement.

He had time—at least three seconds, before Lundy, running alongside the swimming pool, saw him, came to a stop and swung the magnum at him—time to swing the shotgun down and fire and pump and fire again and see Gene Lundy blown off his feet into the swimming pool.

Renda saw that much and knew where the man was down below, knew close enough, and began firing the .45 automatic straight down at the deck boards, concentrating on a small area only a few feet to his left, fired and fired, splintering, gouging the stained wood, and kept firing until the automatic was empty.

He stood listening then. When the gunfire ringing in his ears began to fade, he could hear, very faintly, the sound of hi-fi rock music coming from the main room. That was all. He stepped into the bedroom to reload the .45, still listening, watching the patio—pulling out the clip and throwing it aside, taking another clip from his jacket pocket and smacking it with his palm into the grip.

"Go take a look," Renda said.

Kopas had backed away from the glass doors until the bed stopped him and he felt it against his legs. "Mr. Renda—" He stopped and started over. "The man wasn't running around the side. I was looking, I didn't see him. You told Gene that—you *used* Gene to spot the guy."

Kopas saw him turn and saw his eyes, not looking through him this time but right at him.

"Go downstairs," Renda said, "look out the door. If he's laying there, walk out on the patio. If he isn't laying there, stay where you are."

"I'm sorry," Bobby Kopas said. "I mean I don't even know what I'm *doing* here. I don't give a shit about the guy. Really, it's none of my business. I think I better just—split. You know?" He had to get out, that's all. Just get the hell out of here, though not make it look like he was scared or running. He said, "I'll leave this in case you need it," and dropped the shotgun on the bed as he got around the foot of it and headed for the door.

Renda said, "Bobby—"

Kopas kept going.

He was almost to the stairway when Renda came out into the hall.

"Bobby!"

His hand was on the stair rail. Below him was the open front door and sunlight. He didn't hear his name again. He didn't care if he did. He didn't care now if Renda thought he was running. Just get *out*, that's all.

He got halfway down.

Renda shot him from the top of the stairs, hitting him squarely in the back, twice. Lowering the .45 he saw Kopas lying face-down in the front hall, a few feet from the door, and was aware of the hi-fi music again—a slow rock instrumental—coming from the main room.

All right, he'd go down, go through the room to the patio. Look outside.

Or he could go out the front door and walk around. If the guy was alive he wouldn't know which way he'd be coming from, wouldn't know where to look.

But the guy was probably dead. Or at least hit. He must have hit him. So it didn't matter. Renda moved down the stairs, holding his gaze on the archway below and to the right, that led into the main room. He was at the bottom, in the front hall, about to step over Bobby Kopas's legs, when the hi-fi music stopped. It stopped abruptly, in the middle of the rock number.

Renda waited.

There was no sound from the room. Animal heads looking down in silence at—what? Where would he be? Behind something. Renda could see only part of the room from where he was standing, the windows along the front wall. He would have to walk through the archway to see the rest, not knowing where the guy was. He had never done it like this before, walked in, the guy knowing he was coming. Guy waiting with a shotgun. There was a shotgun upstairs. But if he went up the guy could move again and he wouldn't know where. He knew the guy was in the room. But it was a big room. Or he could be outside again, with the shotgun sticking in the window.

He said to himself, This isn't a fucking game. *Get out.*

Renda went through the doorway, ran across the grass to the Olds 98 and got to it, pulled the door open and started to slide in.

The key wasn't in the ignition.

The fucking key wasn't in the ignition! Lundy had it. No, or it was on the floor . . . or on the dash . . . or on the sun visor. Somewhere!

"Frank?"

Renda came out slowly, turning a little to look over the top of the open door.

Majestyk was standing on the front steps of the house, the shotgun cradled in the crook of his left arm.

"You hear it?" Majestyk said.

Renda turned a little more, keeping the car door

in front of him. He could hear it now, the faint sound of a police siren.

Majestyk waited.

Behind the door, below the window ledge, Renda shifted the .45 automatic in his left hand. He knew he could do it, hit the guy before he moved. Farmboy standing there not knowing it was over. He said, "You want to think about it?"

Majestyk shook his head. "Last chance, Frank."

Renda brought up the .45 automatic, at arm's length out past the edge of the door and fired, trying to aim now as he fired again.

Majestyk swung the shotgun on him and blew out the window in the door, watched Renda stagger out from behind it, still holding the .45 extended, and shot him again, the 12-gauge charge slamming Renda against the side of the car and taking out the rear-door window. Renda went down to his knees, hung there a moment and fell face-down.

Majestyk was sitting on the front steps with the shotgun across his knees. He watched the three squad cars come barreling in through the trees, watched them pull to nose-diving stops and the doors swing open and the deputies come piling out with riot guns and drawn revolvers. They stopped when they saw him and stood there looking around. Lieutenant McAllen walked over.

"You were right," Majestyk said. "That man was trying to kill me."

McAllen looked at him. He didn't say anything. He kept going and walked over to where Renda was lying, stooped down and felt his throat for a pulse. He looked over at Majestyk again.

But Majestyk was walking away, over toward the pickup that had come in behind the squad cars, where the girl was standing.

McAllen watched him put his hand on the girl's shoulder as he opened the door and heard him say, "We'll get us a couple of six-packs on the way home. Right?" And he heard the girl say, "Right." He watched Majestyk's hand slide down to the girl's can as she climbed into the cab and heard her say, "Hey, watch it!" He didn't hear what Majestyk said to her as he slammed the door, but he heard the girl's laughter.

Then Majestyk was walking around the pickup to the driver's side. He looked over and gave McAllen a little wave.

McAllen didn't wave back or say a word. He heard the girl laugh again and watched the pickup drive off through the trees.

RIDING THE RAP
A Raylan Givens Novel
978-0-06-212247-6 (trade paperback)

PRONTO
A Raylan Givens Novel
978-0-06-212033-5 (trade paperback)

RUM PUNCH
978-0-06-211982-7 (trade paperback)

GET SHORTY
978-0-06-212025-0 (trade paperback)

TISHOMINGO BLUES
978-0-06-200939-5 (trade paperback)

KILLSHOT
978-0-06-212159-2 (trade paperback)

FREAKY DEAKY
978-0-06-212035-9 (trade paperback)

BANDITS
978-0-06-212032-8 (trade paperback)

GLITZ
978-0-06-212158-5 (trade paperback)

STICK
978-0-06-218435-1 (trade paperback)

CAT CHASER
978-0-06-219095-6 (trade paperback)

SPLIT IMAGES
978-0-06-212251-3 (trade paperback)

CITY PRIMEVAL
978-0-06-219135-9 (trade paperback)